DOMINIC MORALES

The Next Generation

(The Evolved, Book 1)

To my parents and siblings,
who taught me that a normal family would be boring

Contents

Prologue

"Cassie! You have to run away!" a woman screamed in her dimly lit kitchen.

The few rays of light breaching the shuttered windows illuminated a dire situation in the rustic kitchen. The refined composure of the lone woman there had completely deteriorated. Hands waved wildly. Grunts and incoherent mumbles echoed through the empty home as the woman slammed her head against the wooden countertop. She would give anything to stop the pain, but she could do nothing except grit her teeth and endure the agony.

"Mommy!" a young girl cried out. Her wide eyes watched in horror from behind a door. She felt helpless. The poor girl couldn't leave her room, much less flee her mother. Tears form on the small face consumed by fear. Heavy droplets fell to the ground. Cassie was frozen in place. She wanted to listen to her mother but couldn't. Her body refused to respond properly. She felt cold and hollow. She trembled as she stared at her once graceful mother.

"Get out! Of my…head…" Veronica said between winces. Her order was directed at both her child and whatever was gnawing at her, but neither listened. The mother's thrashing grew more intense as the pain increased. Each tormented second felt like an eternity. Needles were stabbing into her brain as a dark matter ate away at her skin. Veronica's blood boiled and darkened, becoming visible through her fair skin.

Every muscle fiber screamed while being torn from the immense stress and grueling contractions. Bones fractured and joints dislocated as the metamorphosis continued.

Veronica's tolerance had reached its limit. She felt she'd surely perish. Then, much to her surprise, the onslaught of agony ceased. Her darkened hands fell to her side. The pain that had feasted on her soul was replaced with an odd warmth. As the soothing sensation persisted, the dark matter stemmed further along her skin. It crawled underneath her clothing to continue its invasive conquest but, exhausted, she didn't notice. Nothing could break her from the euphoria that now flooded her brain. The limbs that hung lifelessly by her side sank to the ground, stretching like a viscous liquid.

The kitchen fell to a hush. Several moments of silence passed before Cassie let out a sigh of relief. The atmosphere of the room had changed, making it much easier for the child to breathe. Her shoulders slumped as her stress dissipated. The weight of the world had been lifted off her back. The worst of the moment was finally over. Cassie was finally free to leave her room and approach her mother. Tears continued to fall from her cheeks, but joy rushed back to fill her worried heart. Her frigid body could move again. A loving hug to a mother from her child was a warm embrace from Cassie's side, but it wasn't returned in kind.

Cassie assumed it was due to her mother's inner turmoil. Such an attack often left its victims with little energy. It was expected for a person to vegetate for several minutes following a flare-up. The same was true for the black matter that consumed Veronica's flesh. It normally subsided and retreated to its origin point after a short while. Regardless of what form her mother took, Cassie's heart never truly faltered. She always believed that her mother would return to her. Her eyes were full of child-like wonder as she gazed upward. It was amazing to see her heroic mother fight off such a monster. Cassie gave the biggest smile she could muster as she prepared to congratulate her idol.

But the gaze of a predator was the only thing Cassie saw.

The elongated arms rose from their resting positions. They slithered like snakes along the floor. Both approached Cassie with malicious intent. It was a nightmare. It had to be. The young girl once again froze, but there was no one to protect her. She could no longer hide nor run. Whoever she clung to, it wasn't her mother, not anymore. The kind and passionate person she remembered had been replaced by an evil doppelganger.

Despite Veronica's best attempts to resist the transformation, she had finally turned into a Primal. It was now far worse than her previous Fallen state. A sort of instinctive urge was all she could feel. Her higher thought processes completely shut down. Prey was within her reach, and that was all she cared about. Whether the child was previously important to her or not didn't matter. All the Primal wanted was to grab her next meal before it could escape.

Cassie's heart raced as the extended limbs circled her. Each second that passed lowered her chance of a safe retreat. The hands stood inches from her face. They opened and stretched to reveal several internal thorns that formed along the palm and fingers. These two beastly weapons were the perfect tools to catch a child with ease. Cassie's frightened eyes watched in horror as the hands readied for a swift strike that would almost certainly end her life. They lunged forward with extreme prejudice.

Fortunately, the two hands never reached their intended target.

A new set of arms appeared and wrapped around Cassie. Burly hands were coated in a dark red material that had hardened and crystallized. They carefully covered the child and blocked the attack. Nothing could get through such perfectly crafted armor. The new combatant was well-known for his exemplary defense. Not a moment later, Cassie was pulled away from the trap. She gazed up at her knight in shining, shaded crimson, armor.

"Daddy! You're here!" Cassie shouted with joy. Even if the man was veiled with a peculiar material, she knew who it was. The gleam of her father's self-made armor always reminded her of the heroes she'd been told about in stories of an eventful night that took place before she was born. Cassie did not doubt that her father was one of the chevalier heroes. And now, he was her savior, but the battle was far from over. The monstrous mother still occupied the room and was making ready for her next attack. In the best-case scenario, Cassie and her father would make it unscathed. There was no chance to bring Veronica back to her senses, so Cassie's father couldn't consider that a possibility in his analysis.

"Go outside, sweetie. I'll take care of mommy," Orion said to his daughter. Even in this intense situation, he managed to remain calm. He wasn't privy to the best actions to take against a Primal, but it shouldn't be much different from a typical fight between Evolved. Orion prided himself on his armor. The main problem was his daughter. He would need to keep his wife's attention while Cassie escaped the building.

"What's going to happen? Are you going to help?" Cassie said through falling tears and sniffles. She understood the basic symptoms of her mother's affliction but not their full extent. She didn't know it was too late. An intense frost stemmed from her fingers and chilled her entire body. This felt like a final goodbye. Cassie wasn't ready to leave, but she couldn't say those words. She clung to the notion that her father could do something to fix everything, to wake her from her nightmare.

"I'm sorry. Please, go outside. Take Junior, Leo, and Lyra to Aunt Emma's. Tell her 'Nyx has fallen,'" Orion said. He couldn't admit what he was about to do. How could he? Not even he was ready for the death of his wife, and he had known the truth of her sickness for quite some time. The calm father stopped himself from trembling. He couldn't show weakness. It took all of his strength to keep himself from breaking down. The proper actions he needed to take were clear but performing them seemed impossible.

Cassie slowly stepped back. Her feet were as heavy as lead. Each action took a considerable amount of energy and determination. Fear restricted half of her movement. Grief was swiftly consuming the remaining half. Even if she wanted to, Cassie couldn't move. She wasn't ready. Her body refused to run away. Tears continued to fall from Cassie's cheeks. Incoherent apologies escaped her mouth as the child repented in a desperate attempt to make everything right. She felt crushed.

And so, she was an easy target.

The snake-like hands rose and flailed once again as the Primal Veronica readied herself. She took several steps forward to allow her arms a greater reach. Hissing escaped the extended limbs and more serrated thorns burst through her flesh. A stream of noxious smoke rose from the dark matter. Veronica was changing, more than she normally could. Her body was mutating to better fit her deteriorating mental state. With an armored man in front of her, she needed to increase her combative capabilities. Every part of her changed to better kill her husband. In a single moment, the family's life was changed forever.

The darkened hands launched toward the young girl, scarring her for the rest of her life.

Chapter 1: Void

A soft breeze blew in from the north, causing autumn leaves to dance in the air. It was a chilly October morning for the citizens of Polus. The surrounding area rarely got temperatures as cold as this so early in the year, so it wasn't surprising to see the city's residents overcompensate with thick jackets and multiple layers. Contrasting the natives, tourists and out-of-state students found the weather delightful. It was yet one more way that Polus found itself divided.

One of the few unifying aspects of the city was its love of coffee. The caffeinated substance was in high demand by both working adults and struggling students. New blends and flavors were devoured immediately, and it wasn't uncommon to hear loud disputes over the city's best shops. The competition was fierce. Merchants had to do whatever they could to maintain public attention. The most successful of them all was Animate Cafe.

It was a moderately sized establishment that sat across the street from the local community college. Students and professors frequently dropped by to receive their morning fixes before class. They love the escapism atmosphere of the cafe. The walls displayed wheels of film and images of important icons of animation history. Both animations and the menu above the main counter flickered as an old projector would. This environment heavily contrasted with the high-tech world around it. Most customers were surprised when they first entered the building. It was like stepping back into a simpler time, a way to get away from the ever-evolving world outside the walls.

As usual on a Friday morning, the cafe was packed with customers. Many were forced to stand, waiting for a seat. It was rare to find an empty table at this hour. One lucky group only managed to get their seats in a corner booth because they knew one of the employees. They didn't want to spend a favor owed to them, but the four customers needed to discuss something important. One of them was having an extremely hard time, and the struggle was written on their face.

The group was split into male and female pairs with the younger couple sitting against the far wall. The young man sat in the corner with a relaxed pose. His oversize sweatshirt and unkempt dark brown hair exemplified a nonchalant aura. Tired hazel eyes remained locked on his phone as the conversation started. At a glance, he didn't seem interested in what the group was discussing, but looks were often deceiving in that way. Mentally, he was already several steps ahead of his peers.

His companion, a woman about a year younger than himself, had a similar countenance. The main difference between the two was that his appearance came from apathy while hers was of distress. Her tired almond eyes stared far beyond the window next to their table. A prominent scar made a straight line from the edge of her left eye to her ear, and another scar slid down her right cheek to the base of her neck. Exhausted, the young woman used her arms as pillows and rested her head on the table. The bulk of her wavy dark brown hair dangled off the table's edge.

The older pair was dressed much more professionally than their casual counterparts. With eyes matching the hue of the coffee she yearned for, the woman had the warm and glowing demeanor of a person one could easily talk to. Dressed in medical scrubs, she was ready to start her day at the local clinic. Light gleamed off the gold feather pendant hanging around her neck. She twirled a strand of long black hair as she thought about what to say next. This conversation was rather delicate, so she didn't want to mention anything that would make the situation worse.

Compared to the lovely woman, the man was frigid as the arctic. Stylistically, however, he was the most put together of the four. His black hair was cleanly cut, and his outfit radiated an official presence. An expensive-looking silver watch sat snugly on his wrist and perfectly complimented his appearance. His eyes matched his partner's in color but not emotion. They were narrow and analytical. Occasionally, he'd nod to acknowledge what was said. Any reply he gave was short and to the point.

"Ah, this sucks," the young woman, Cassie, said. She let out a moan. It was obvious that she was tired, but remedying her current affliction was much more complicated than simply going to sleep. Her nightly routine was only getting worse as each day passed. Whatever sleep she did manage to get was limited. Classes and assignments waited for no one, and her issue was destroying the rest she'd normally get at night.

"So, you had another nightmare about mom?" The older man, Leo, reiterated what he was told earlier in the conversation. He felt sorry for his little sister. Experiencing such an event as Cassie had at a young age wasn't something he would wish on his worst enemy. A type of survivor's guilt clung to her still, haunting her. Her three siblings could never fully understand what happened that day. They were all outside the house while she witnessed the event firsthand. Leo felt awful he couldn't help. As one of the oldest, it was up to him to be a solid foundation for the four siblings.

"Sweetie, these dreams of yours are happening more often than before. Maybe we should schedule you to see a psychiatrist?" the older woman, Lyra, finally said.

Much like her twin brother Leo, she was also upset that she couldn't do anything. The two held precarious positions within the family. It was embarrassing for them to fail in such a way. They each felt they should have noticed the issue with Cassie long before it grew to this scale. Only one other time came to mind when Lyra felt this useless. It was right after their mother's death. The road to recovery was a long one for Cassie, and she had difficulties letting other people in. Thankfully, she managed to stabilize for a few years with the help of family and some close friends, but something had happened recently that sparked the renewal of her trauma.

"I already found a few." The young man, Orion, showed his phone screen to the others. The top half of the screen displayed a map of the city with several marked locations. Each icon was given one of three colors depending on its location. To no one's surprise, the red icons were the cheapest and appeared less frequently than the lavish green ones. The prices ranged wildly, as did the ratings. Further details were displayed on the bottom half of the screen. Of course, the siblings wanted to give Cassie the best treatment available, but the green locations were out of the question for several reasons.

"Thanks, but I've got this covered. We can't be wasting money on something as stupid as this," Cassie said. Her desire to be self-sufficient was the only reason she rejected the help. She never liked being coddled, especially after living most of her life between therapy sessions. If anyone was going to find a solution to her problem, it would be herself. That was why she waited months before telling her family about the resurgence of her nightmares. The family's current financial predicament was simply a good excuse that no one could refute.

"You're right. We don't have the funds," Leo said with a dejected look. As one of the two adults in the family with full-time jobs, he felt responsible for the dire situation the four found themselves in. They couldn't afford to give the medical treatment that Cassie clearly needed. Even Cassie, who was suffering from nightmares and sleep deprivation, recognized that the costs were too great. There was only one option to find help without breaking the bank.

"So, you're going to talk to Aunt Emma about this," Leo said.

"What? No way. Aunt Emma is so weird. Just talking to her gives me a headache. Why can't we get Uncle Brent? Even Morgan would be better if I had to pick." Cassie said, unfairly targeting her irritation toward her aunt. Emma had an interesting speech pattern and rarely expressed any emotion. Her permanently neutral face and voice were off-putting. The way she became engrossed in her thoughts and marched to the beat of her own drum only added to their relative's interesting nature.

"Try not to be rude to our aunt, sweetheart. She's unique in her own way like all…" Lyra was interrupted by their server.

"Hear ye. Hear ye. The coffee fairy hath arrived. Dost thou sleepy head need a second drink for thine departure?" Sadie, one of the cafe's baristas, held a tray full of drinks. She was the close friend that reserved the table for the family of four. Her cheerful nature and playful theatrical entrance were a stark contrast from her best friend, Cassie. The two couldn't be any more different at that moment. One was a gloomy brunette that appeared to be a visible mess. The other was a vibrant blond with an award-winning smile and stunning blue eyes.

"Oh, hey Sadie. I'm good, thanks," Cassie said without moving.

She didn't have the energy to greet her friend properly. The limitless glee that spilled out of Sadie was obnoxious at certain hours of the day. Even if the two were close, Cassie wasn't in the mood for the usual banter. Not until she had some caffeine in her system.

"Wow. I give you a sneak peek into the Drama Club's upcoming play, and all I get is an 'oh, hey Sadie'. Come on, what do I got to do to turn that frown upside down?" Sadie said with a smile. Her joy was annoying to deal with so early in the morning, but it was also infectious. It didn't take long for everyone to start smiling. Even Cassie fell victim to the group's sudden mood shift. Sadie had managed to lift the group's grim atmosphere without much effort. Unfortunately, it would also be her that would immediately ruin everything, "Well, I better get back to work. You guys better have a great day."

Sadie gave Leo a quick kick before pulling up her sleeve and tapping her wrist at him. Thorny vine-like lines wrapped around her arm. The dark markings started at the base of her hand and slowly swirled as they crept up her forearm. This was her Emblem. It was a symbol that identified her as a member of a certain subset of people. Additional rules and discrimination came with the presence of such markings. Thankfully, Sadie's work uniform was long-sleeved, so it wasn't a problem for her. The same couldn't be said about Orion, who let his Emblem be exposed for all to see.

Leo's gaze darted between Sadie's exposed Emblem and her ever-present smile. He immediately got the hint and scoffed. It was clear that the initial playful banter was used to cushion the blow that was just dealt. Sadie may have seemed carefree and easygoing, but she could be awfully crafty when she needed to be. Leo looked around the cafe for a brief moment. It didn't take long to see that a group of elderly individuals was glaring at them.

"Seriously?" Orion said before letting out an irritated sigh. The situation wasn't out of the norm for the family, but its timing was awful. He partially blamed himself for allowing his Emblem to be exposed to the wrong types of people. Many people got angry just by gazing at these imperfections and looked down on those that possessed them. Society still needed time to snuff out that type of prejudice. After all, it had only been around twenty years since Emblems and those who wore them made their debut.

"Sorry, but we ought to get out of here," Leo apologized to his family. They had preferred to stay longer, but that was no longer an option. The best solution was for the four to admit defeat and leave. Fighting the issue and attempting to stay would only cause more problems than it was worth.

"Leo's right. Work starts soon for us, and you two need to get to school," Lyra said, trying to justify their reason for departing early. True, she and her brother had full-time jobs, but Orion and Cassie were college students. Their schedules were extremely flexible, and Animate Cafe was across the street from campus.

"It's fine. Professor Woz asked to speak with me, so I shouldn't be late. Who knows, maybe it'll help clear my head," Cassie said as she rose from her seat. A last heavy gulp of coffee restored some of her diminished vitality. The bags under her eyes seemed a tad bit lighter. The talk had been short, but it helped. She still resented how much she was depending on the others. It made her feel inferior in a way. Like she couldn't handle her own issues without someone else's help. Everyone in her family had grown up in their own way, yet Cassie continued to lag behind. Burying her growing complex, Cassie prepared to leave.

"Yeah. I should be heading back to the *Red Zone.* You know, where I belong. With all the other monsters," Orion said. He projected his voice for everyone else to hear. He couldn't mask his irritation but refused to stoop to the level of the elderly group. Nothing would have satisfied him more than telling them off, but he wasn't confident enough to do that. Plus, he didn't want to cause problems for the others. Orion considered the teaching of his late father, pick your battle.

The silent siblings nodded to one another and proceeded to leave. They accepted the situation and held their heads high. The elderly people smiled over their minuscule victory. A polite wave was given to Sadie before the four departed. Her previously cheerful nature had been replaced with dejection, but it was hard to tell at a glance. The false smile that remained often fooled those that didn't know her true nature.

⠄⠇⠒⠇⠀⠇⠇⠄⠂⠒

Polaris Community College was a small campus relative to the nearby university. There was always a perceived notion that the Green Zone received more funding than the Red Zone. It wasn't a well-kept secret. Polaris's construction revealed the truth. The college was built in an area colloquially referred to as the "Orange Zone," an area of the Yellow Zone that suffered from Red Zone issues. As a result, Polaris was only given the most basic of facilities and limited staff. It wasn't anywhere near the level of prestige that the university had. Despite this, it was still able to provide a decent education to those that attended.

Cassie immediately split off from her family. The cafe they left acted as a center point to meet before the four siblings went their separate ways. Orion returned to the Red Zone to sleep before his afternoon classes. Lyra followed her younger brother into the same zone and started her shift at the local clinic. Leo remained in the Yellow Zone alongside Cassie but had to travel in a different direction to reach the high school where he taught.

The walk to campus turned out to be more insightful than expected. Cassie thought about the correct action to take. Part of her regretted speaking about her nightmares in the first place. If she kept quiet, her siblings' concern would have been nonexistent. Everything could have proceeded as normal. Cassie could simply blame her studies on lack of sleep. No one would be any wiser. It was certainly better than having everyone walk on eggshells at the sheer mention of nightmares. She scoffed. It wasn't as if Primals caused her to freeze in place. Even if they did, Polus had been Primal-free for quite some time. It was odd that their presence had suddenly dwindled in the past few years, but Cassie wasn't going to question it.

That is until she walked into a gruesome scene.

Police tape marked off a section of the road. A car was tossed on its side. Its skyward-facing doors were torn open with prominent claw marks etched into the exterior. The white outline of a body sat next to the crash site. The road was broken in several spots where something incredibly heavy smashed into it. The surrounding buildings were broken into and splattered with blood and a black liquid. Smaller white outlines were placed randomly around the scene, marking the points where loose body parts fell. The victor was the sole survivor, but they didn't leave unscathed. A large blood trail traced the person's path as it headed toward the Red Zone. Evolved rarely fought each other due to the mutually assured destruction that came with it, but Cassie imagined this was what it would look like. No, this was far from a standard fight.

This was the work of a Primal.

Cassie felt herself lock in place. Her hands shook violently. Her face paled. Her core temperature dropped considerably. A chill went down her spine before her entire back heated as if preparing to fight or flee. She stared at the scene for several minutes. A worrying thought echoed in her mind. It slowly multiplied with additional scenarios, compounding with impossible factors that eventually resulted in the worst outcome. Each moment felt like an eternity. The Primal wasn't even here and yet she was terrified of its presence. What would happen if she collided with it? Would she also be defeated and devoured?

Cassie shook her head. She turned on her heels and hastily walked away from the scene. She'd much rather take the longer alternative route than follow her previous one. She immediately tried to drown out her negative thoughts. Cassie's pace increased, almost to a complete sprint. She focused on the task ahead. Her professor explicitly asked for her attendance in a one-on-one meeting. That was all she needed to worry about.

Cassie was familiar with her teacher, Professor Woz. The two couldn't be considered friends, but they did have a mutual acquaintance. Despite this moderate relationship, Cassie felt uneasy about the meeting. She'd never been called into a teacher's office before. Any messages between the two were through e-mail and were kept professional. What had she done wrong to the point that a meeting was required? Cassie took a deep breath to calm her thoughts. Now that the scene was in the distance, she managed to stabilize herself. She paused to steel her mind before cautiously entering the lion's den.

Inside the office sat a middle-aged woman in a lab coat. Large glasses rested on the bridge of her nose, and her short curly hair bobbed as she nodded to the jazz playing from her phone. She wore a pink turtleneck beneath her outerwear, so it was impossible to see if she had an Emblem. Even if it couldn't be seen, Cassie knew her teacher lacked those types of markings.

Violet Woz was a resident of the Green Zone and one of the few people brave enough to enter the Red Zone. As per regulations, special permission was needed for her to access a zone not intended for her. It was an arduous process, so she only ever entered when she wanted to meet with a friend at his establishment. It was why she enjoyed teaching at Polaris. She was able to encounter denizens of the Red Zone without needing to go through the hassle of physically entering the zone.

Contrasting the put-together professor, the office was a chaotic mess. It was next to impossible to find anything on the cluttered desk. Student work and research articles were mixed and shuffled. Open books and peer-reviewed studies were bookmarked and sprawled out for the reader's convenience. The computer desktop managed to be even worse with its swarm of icons linking to text files and submitted projects. The only person that could operate in this environment was Violet.

No one knew how she managed to work two jobs in two separate zones, but they couldn't argue with the results. Violet was famous for her innovations in technology and biochemistry. Her contributions to the development of Red Zones across the country also made her extremely popular. In the past, she was offered numerous positions from other companies and universities but opted to remain in Polus.

She wanted nothing more than to help the city and finish her research there. The city's proximity to her hometown also swayed her decision.

"Have a seat," Violet said, breaking the initial awkward silence. She spoke with a soft voice that eased Cassie's worries. A polite hand gestured to the recently emptied seat across from her. It was calming yet seemed oddly forced, as if Violet had been practicing the motion to seem more professional.

"Is there something wrong?" Cassie asked as she sat down.

She was concerned about several things. A large paper was due recently. Exams were around the corner. The final date to withdraw was fast approaching. It was also around this time that the more senior students began volunteering at some of the college's partner companies. The number of things Violet could bring up was endless, and Cassie was sent spiraling.

"That's what I was going to ask you. You seem to be having difficulties focusing in class," Violet said with a soothing voice.

Cassie felt a mental sigh of relief. Her grade wasn't on the line. Slumped shoulders gave away the fact that Cassie's tension had been released.

Violet took the opportunity to reassure her student, "Aside from you looking like you sprinted here in terror, there's nothing explicitly wrong. I just want to talk about whatever has been bothering you. Speaking with a detached stranger may be easier than speaking to family. Although, if you want to, I suppose we could address you sleeping in class."

Ah, so that's how it is, Cassie thought.

She avoided her professor's eyes and quietly fixed her hair. She felt embarrassed over the situation. It seemed like everyone could see that she had a problem. Everyone wanted to offer their help. Everyone had to give their insight. No answer was ever good enough to push these people away. Cassie felt overwhelmed. She could solve her own problems. She *had* to solve them on her own.

So, Cassie gave the most generic answer she could. "Thanks, Professor Woz, but I'm fine."

"Trust me. I've gone through years of therapy and saying 'I'm fine'. That said, I won't force anything. We can just talk about improving your sleeping habits."

Violet's words were sincere, more than any she had ever said in the past. That was because they came from experience. Violet knew what it was like to feel lost and alone. She had battled her demons and fears long ago. Unsurprisingly, Cassie had never heard of her professor's problems. Everyone had their own issues, but she always assumed Violet was above that.

"I'm surprised to hear that," Cassie said out of curiosity.

She was interested in her teacher's problems and how they related to herself. Violet wouldn't have brought it up without a reason, but it wasn't likely that she had faced anything similar to Cassie's past trauma. Primals were rarely an issue for people like Violet. Both Fallen and Primals were extremely uncommon in Yellow Zones across the nation, and Green Zones had virtually zero issues. Today's scene would likely be resolved immediately, or it would be completely ignored if the Primal was suspected of retreating into the Red Zone. Only Cassie's home, the Red Zone, had these common troubles.

"Well, not everyone is a survivor from the Night of A Thousand Blades. My parents weren't so lucky, though. I guess those monsters had a soft side for me," Violet said.

She tried to form her words as a playful joke, but it was impossible. That event was far too serious to be taken lightly. It wasn't a secret that most students attending Polaris were related to the night's masked participants. It was even possible for Violet to have taught the children of her parents' murderers without any knowledge of their real identities. The thought was a conflicting one, to say the least, so Violet never explored it.

"I see," Cassie said under her breath.

She flinched at the word monsters. The night mentioned happened about a year before she was born and had an intense dual perspective. One side, which consisted entirely of people like Violet, saw the masked people as monsters and criminals. The opposing view, held by people like Cassie, held them as heroes and champions. Regardless of opinion, the facts were clear. One thousand people were targeted on a certain night, and none survived. Most details behind the perpetrators were hidden behind masks, lies, and treaties.

"I'm not trying to downplay your problem. Just know that others have gone through similar experiences, and my door is always open," Violet emphasized her last point. She wanted her students to depend on her. They were all young minds that held a heavy weight and aspired to uphold their own legacy.

"If I'm not mistaken, your current research project revolves around Fallen and Primals, right?" Cassie asked.

Talking about her issues was difficult, so Cassie chose to do so in a roundabout way. The scene from earlier was also still fresh in her mind, which further drove her into believing this was the right topic to discuss. It may have been best to learn more about her phobia from a legitimate researcher. The answers provided would be more reliable than anything Cassie would find in her own investigation. Of course, there were an infinite number of topics that were better than talking about how Cassie's mother tried to kill her as a child.

"Yes. Legally and ethically speaking, I cannot say anything new until my current study concludes. All that I can say is that Fallen are the precursors to Primals. What makes an Evolved turn into a Fallen then subsequent Primal is still unknown, as is the exact transition time." Violet said it with a straight voice. Her words were concise and to the point as if she were reading to avoid breaking her non-disclosure agreement. That limited response didn't provide anything helpful. It was general knowledge that the public already knew.

"That makes sense. I look forward to reading what your team publishes. Isn't Reggie working with you on that front?" Cassie asked.

She knew the conversation had reached its peak. Cassie would have to either discuss her past or shift the topic. The option was clear. She wanted nothing to do with exposing her problems. Fortunately, the common acquaintance that Cassie and Violet shared acted as an excellent segue.

"He is. I find his devotion to the project to be inspiring, but I also find your topic change to be impressive," Violet said with a sly smile. The earnest attempt to avoid dealing with the pressing issue brought back memories of her own past attempts. Violet fondly remembered how her therapist loathed the excuses and random topics chosen to talk about anything other than her problems. Still, she was a woman of her word. "Look, if you truly believe you can solve your issues without assistance, you can handle this on your own. It's your prerogative. I do, however, recommend you read some of the self-help articles written by Julia Norris."

"Understood. Thanks for taking the time to help me." Cassie nodded before standing up. She made a mental note of the famous author that wrote several articles after the Night of A Thousand Blades. Maybe something would help? Cassie gave a slight bow as she left the office.

She couldn't stop herself from being stubborn. Thoughts of alternatives flooded her mind, but they weren't any better than what had already been suggested. Did she need professional help? No. Cassie could handle everything on her own, like a proper adult. There had to be another option. One that didn't take advantage of the numerous people who were eager to help. It seemed like everyone wanted to assist.

All but one person.

"You're here early. Came to cry about the paper you plagiarized?" A nonchalant woman said as she approached Cassie.

This tall and relaxed person was Audrey, a freelance computer programmer that often worked for the college. She was dressed in casual wear, and a messenger bag hung from her shoulder. Her Emblem took the form of a large circle that covered her chest, but only the top part of it could be seen along her collarbone. The exposed portion was enough to show that her Emblem was hollow and resembled an outline. Disheveled amber hair stopped just above her shoulders and showed that she had only woken up recently. Her tired emerald eyes complemented the exhausted appearance that she didn't care to hide.

"I wish. Professor Woz wanted to know what was wrong with me." Cassie sulked.

She tapped the seat next to her, but Audrey didn't take advantage of her kindness, preferring to stand because her job had her sitting a lot. Cassie knew her friend would reject her. The two had been friends since high school, along with the barista Sadie. It was why Cassie could predict that Audrey wouldn't sit and have a serious conversation with her. That was one of Audrey's charms.

"You mean, aside from the whole no parents thing?" Audrey said playfully.

The relationship between the two was extremely casual, and they often made fun of each other as friends would. Of course, some things shouldn't have been the subject of mocking, but Cassie never seemed bothered by it. Enough time had passed to the point that some of those wounds could be joked about. It was only because of recent events that Cassie was less enthusiastic about the usual banter.

"Something like that. Nightmares and whatnot. Plus, two of my friends are going on a date this weekend and the other won't answer my texts. So, nothing but negatives today," Cassie said with a slight laugh.

She knew Audrey wouldn't coddle her as the others did. Unless it was said with a serious voice, every word was fair game to make light of. There was no need to hide her issues because her friend wouldn't investigate. This type of conversation was a delightful change of pace. Casually speaking to a friend without worry was just what Cassie needed. Unfortunately, the chat would be cut short. Audrey had a job to do.

"As much as I'd love to hear about what goes bump in the night, I have to get to work. People will think I'm unprofessional if I show up late. I'll make it up to you next time," Audrey said.

She tapped her bag to emphasize her point. She was great at her job and often finished faster than expected. It was the main reason people hired her. The low prices she set were also hard to beat. Audrey's reputation was impossible to surpass. There was no end to the number of businesses that tried to compete with her. Even with her unknown malpractice.

"Maybe we can just meet at the Oasis tonight?" Cassie asked a hopeful question.

Friday nights were meant to be enjoyed, but Audrey and Sadie had missed the last few weeks. Cassie was starting to miss her friends despite seeing them almost every day. Casual greetings were nothing compared to a night together. This only became more problematic with their conflicting schedules.

"Nope. Tomorrow's date night, so I can't be going out, getting drunk, and wasting money before that. I can't stand another lecture about personal responsibility even with that pretty smile. Guess that means you'll have to drink my share. Maybe it'll help with those dreams of yours. If not, come to my place." Audrey gave a casual wave before walking off.

The encounter was typical for the duo, yet it still left Cassie confused. Was that supposed to be advice or another stupid joke? Cassie often had a hard time deciphering Audrey's true intention. Classes were about to start, so playing detective would have to wait for another time.

The sun set as the day waned. The streets were packed with people trying to return home. Restaurants filled with the wave of dinner rush diners. Kitchen staff, bartenders, and waiters alike dreaded this time of day. Orders came flying in as the scarcity of empty tables increased. Everyone worked together like a well-oiled machine to feed the city. Most restaurants in both the Yellow Zone and Green Zone had to work this way. Businesses boomed in these areas due to their larger and wealthier populations. Outsmarting competitors was the only way to stay on top within such volatile markets.

Comparatively, the Red Zone was barren. Restaurants were often vacant and wasted more money than they generated. Infrastructure was limited and compressed. Construction was slow due to improper funding, so it was common for new businesses to start on the remnants of old ones. To save money, they frequently opened late or closed early. The only places that saw relative success were those along the Red-Yellow Zone border. The number of active businesses took a noticeable drop after leaving the area. It was considered financially irresponsible to try any ventures deeper into the zone, so most avoided it.

All except for one small bar near the zone's center.

Fee's Oasis was a narrow building, squished between taller complexes. From an outside perspective, it was an incredibly small establishment, but looks were often deceiving. Its depth was remarkable and caught new customers off-guard. Guests were immediately greeted by the sight of a small kitchen along the left wall. It was shielded by curved glass that allowed consumers to watch their meal be made. As the building continued, the elongated kitchen slowly morphed into a well-designed bar. Numerous bottles of liquor lined the shelves, and a soft light gave them a glowing appearance.

A mix of tables and booths made up the dining area along the right side of the restaurant. Images of the three owners, family friends, and frequent customers hung on the walls alongside sports memorabilia and news articles. The wooden paneled walls and dark oak furniture gave the room a rustic and relaxing atmosphere. Every table had old newspapers and pictures displayed under wood stain and sealant. Adding to the ambiance of Fee's Oasis was a grand piano in the far corner. During less active times, one of the three staff members would play a song at the customer's request.

While the bar received many patrons throughout the night, the staff was always limited. This was because the restaurant was run solely by its owners. The Dorado brothers were a set of triplets who handled all the tasks necessary to keep the family business going. Each operated to fulfill the customer's needs. Normally, this reduced staff would have resulted in less than five-star quality service, but that was never an issue. The three brothers worked together like a well-oiled machine and earnestly tried to satisfy anyone who walked through the main doors.

Due to the brothers' obvious similarities, they remained in their respective areas to avoid confusion. They wore slight variations of the main uniform to assist people in identifying the three. The base of the uniform was rather generic: a white button-up dress shirt with rolled sleeves, black slacks, and a tie. The key difference in the uniforms was the vest they wore. It also helped that their Emblems were varied.

The eldest brother, Reggie, wore a crimson vest. Rigid black lines reached symmetrically from his fingers to his torso. Despite looking like the others, he seemed tougher than his brothers. It was his job to maintain the bar and use various liquors to create mixed drinks. Most of his free time was spent polishing glasses and cleaning his area, but there was rarely a shortage of weary souls that needed a quick fix. While the bar had many specialty drinks, most customers opted for beer from the local breweries.

The middle brother, Jack, wore a navy vest. The markings along his arms were much more jagged compared to Reggie's. They twisted and jolted along his skin, and small thorns emboldened the Emblem's silhouette. Even with his naturally dark complexion, the lines prominently stood out. Fortunately, exposing his Emblem wasn't a problem in the Red Zone. Jack was able to take orders, keep drinks full, and clean tables without any issues. He also happened to be the most sociable of the three and was the primary piano player.

The youngest brother, Francis, wore a forest green vest. Unlike his two brothers, he had no lines along his arms. Instead, his Emblem took the form of numerous small triangles. Each one was about the size of a coin, and they all pointed toward his extremities. Francis also had another major difference that further separated him from the others. His right arm was noticeably missing. In its place was an artificial limb that connected to his nervous system and operated just as well as its biological counterpart. He had no trouble working in the kitchen alone. The simple menu and low volume of customers meant that Francis rarely felt stress from his duties.

Together, the Dorado brothers were able to provide a pleasant experience to any customer that entered Fee's Oasis. One such set of customers was a familiar group of four. They were frequent diners and personal friends of the triplets. The family ate their burgers and wings while watching the news, and locally brewed IPAs filled their half-empty glasses. It was probably the best way to watch the anchorman as he delivered important information. The Lee family came every Friday night when the restaurant experienced a significant drop in customers. Usually, they'd watch whatever sports team Jack placed a bet on, but that wasn't an option tonight. Having served the group, the Dorado brothers sat at a nearby table and the conversation unfolded.

"So, a little bird told me you guys got the boot from Animate Cafe," Francis said with a coy smile.

There was no gentle way to bring up the subject, so he decided to frame it as a joke. Scenarios like the one he had been told weren't uncommon. That wasn't to say they were legal either, but fighting the issue would only ruin a person's public image. It was the main reason this type of problem continued. People from the Green Zone had less to lose than those from the Red Zone. It also didn't help that local law enforcement and their superior division, the Enforcers, weren't keen on helping.

"I'm guessing that bird told you that with her face in her hands or slammed against a pillow," Orion replied sarcastically. In protest of what happened earlier in the day, he had taken off his sweatshirt to put his arms on full display. The three lines that flowed along his forearms were much more obvious. It was easy to see that the two outer markings followed his radius and ulna bones while the central one cut straight through the middle.

"Don't be mean. That poor girl had to continue working after we left. I'm sure she got hit with a bunch of nasty looks, if not slurs," Lyra said. Much like her brother, she wasn't covering her Emblem. Her work attire had been replaced with a casual outfit which now exposed her once hidden markings. A mysterious web-like formation covered both of her elbows and branched out like fractured glass. They didn't stretch far from their origin point and ended with a sharp tip.

"Yeah, they've been getting creative lately. I'm kind of impressed with what I've heard. Almost brings a tear to my eye," Jack said. He cackled as he reminisced about what he had been called that week. Name-calling wasn't an oddity within the Yellow Zone. Much like refusing service, it was technically illegal to do so, but not many were willing to enforce that law.

An obvious level of disdain was present between the residents of the Red Zone and the Green Zone. The Yellow Zone just happened to be the common ground where spats could occur. This was true for every city or county that implemented zoning laws.

"You guys think it's bad? Try going to the other side. That place is hell for folks like us," Reggie said while leaning back in his chair. Out of all seven friends present, he was the only person that was permitted to enter the Green Zone. His work as a researcher gave him that special privilege to access the monumental university and its array of facilities. Of course, that exception wasn't enough to make everything perfect. Despite his enhanced permissions, Reggie was subjected to numerous tests at the zone's checkpoints before entering each day. Enforcers could stop him whenever they wanted, and he had to wear a special bracelet that marked him as an out-of-place individual.

The news continued to play ominously in the background. Most of the group was keeping an ear out for anything important. There was a critical piece of legislation that was expected to be presented that day. The first draft was leaked to the public and resulted in major backlash from numerous parties. What was suggested was borderline ludicrous. It was like a bad joke, yet truth seemed to be stranger than fiction. The day's grim results were announced on live television.

"How the Anti-Armament Law is supposed to hold in court is beyond me. Not to mention how they shoved in the clause that increases the Enforcer budget," Francis said. As a man of law, he was able to identify the new legislation as a constitutional infringement from its infancy.

Then again, that was just how politics worked. Every action was superficial and radical. If it didn't work, politicians would blame the opposing party and attempt to pass something even worse. If it did, another grisly night was bound to happen like the one from twenty years prior. Regardless, the community was bound to experience turbulence in the coming years.

Jack laughed. "Good luck with that. My Armament can't exactly be turned off. Well…not all the way. Plus, the Enforcers are complete garbage. All the AE equipment in the world couldn't save them from themselves, let alone actual threats. Anyone that gets beaten by them is either extraordinarily weak, distracted, or sucker-punched," he said.

Armaments varied from person to person. It was next to impossible to limit them all, especially those that were passive like Jack's and Reggie's.

Both drinks and food alike rapidly disappeared as everyone enjoyed the last few hours of the night. Their banter continued and arguments were started over the new law's logistics. Refills were eagerly demanded, and the Dorado brothers happily obliged. The friends progressed from slightly buzzed to mildly inebriated as time passed. The four customers gave their approval of their meals. Some did so more than others.

"These guys are s-so good," Cassie said with a slurred voice. She stared at the extra order of seasoned fries before her. Glazed eyes looked far beyond the side dish as she became engrossed in her slow thoughts. As the smallest and youngest of the seven, it wasn't surprising to see her state of mind after trying to keep pace with the others. Cassie grabbed one of the many fries and nibbled on it. Tiny bites continued while she quietly rocked herself.

To no one's surprise, Cassie's excessive rocking forced her off-balance. She tilted further back than intended and was sent reeling. Her reaction speed had been slowed considerably, so all she could do was fall. The sluggish movements she could perform weren't enough to save herself. For the briefest of moments, Cassie felt the world slow as she descended. The hardwood floor inched closer and engrossed her field of vision.

Then, all of Cassie's downward momentum halted in an instant.

Dazed and confused, Cassie looked around for an answer. It was then that she saw an interesting sight. Her eyes blinked several times as if to process what had happened. She tilted her head toward her seatmate, Leo. He was looking over his shoulder at his drunken sister.

A sigh escaped him, but it wasn't clear if it came from exhaustion or annoyance. He did have a long day at work. Teaching high schoolers didn't come easy. He'd made sure to tell his sister to watch her alcohol intake after a similar experience the previous week.

Cassie steeled herself for the inevitable lecture that was to come. She avoided eye contact and focused on the line that connected her to her brother.

Leo's overall demeanor remained unchanged. He was the same relatively silent and insightful man he always was. It was as if he hadn't even noticed the odd bone structure protruding from his back. This perplexing object was, in fact, his spine. His entire backbone reached out of his lower back and curved toward Cassie's chair. A grotesque dark vine connected each vertebra, ending with an unnaturally edged tail bone. The matter had a slight sheen like metal and softly pulsated in a rhythmic pattern. The gaps between each vertebra varied in length as the entire formation stretched to catch Cassie. Having done its job, the spine receded back to its original biological position.

Cassie sat back as her seat slowly rose, thanks to her brother's tail. The monstrous structure that saved her eventually escaped her field of vision. She was still in shock over what had happened. Not her brother's sudden generation of a new appendage. That wasn't what startled her. It was common for an Evolved to use their Armament. Instead, Cassie was bewildered by her level of intoxication. She thought she could handle herself better. She knew she needed to apologize for making a scene and properly thank her brother, but her mind was still hazy. Slow lips tried to open and speak, only to be immediately interrupted.

"Wow. Nice catch, Leo. You're pretty quick for someone that's been drinking all night," Jack said with a smile. He nodded his head in approval.

Leo was probably the only person that could pull a stunt like that.

It was one of the many reasons Jack respected him so much. Red Zone residents, the Evolved, valued two things above all else: power and integrity. Of course, the former was incredibly flexible given the variety of Armaments an Evolved could be born with. The latter was practically drilled into every mind at an early age, forming a mutual trust amongst the entire populace.

"I was just gonna say that. He got me, an-an-and he didn't even scratch the chair," Cassie said louder than she intended to. She rubbed her chair, impressed by both its durability and Leo's level of consideration in the heat of the moment. Her eyes locked on the fry she dropped during the movement. A quiet huff escaped her as she pouted. It was a waste. Her intoxicated mind regretted the final result. If she had one more beer in her system, she would have likely bawled over the fallen French fry.

"What can I say? I'm a pro. Been doing it for years," Leo said with a smile. His quick Armament saved his siblings more times than he could count. A sense of nostalgia filled him as he thought back to the family's golden years, back when the world made sense and their parents were still alive. Those warm memories quickly dissipated once Leo noticed his younger sister's longing gaze at the ground. He placed a hand on her head as if to stop her. He let out a soft chuckle. "We should get out of here before you decide to clean the floors for free."

"Thank you for the night. Stay safe out there, especially now that we might be getting more Enforcers. And that other issue…" Lyra said, mumbling her final words so that Cassie couldn't hear them, before standing up. She kept her drinking to a minimum, and it showed. Her movements were much more graceful and controlled than the others. She and Francis were often the ones who drank less within their respective families. Lyra quietly dug through her purse and retrieved a credit card. She handed it to her sober companion, and the two walked off to complete the transaction.

"Yeah. You take care of yourself, too. Don't hesitate to call if you need anything. Especially with those weird masked people running around," Francis replied while avoiding eye contact. He alluded to the rumor floating around town about a group of vigilantes, but Lyra probably wasn't worried about that. She was gifted with a strong Armament and often practiced martial arts to get her mind off things. If anything, Lyra should have been the last person that Francis worried about. He'd be better off focusing on himself. His missing arm meant that his Armament's total power was cut in half. Comparing the two was like comparing night and day, yet Francis would never stop worrying about the woman that captured his heart.

Lyra, none the wiser of her friend's true feelings, gave a polite smile before grabbing her belongings and departing with the others. The usual familial banter was now enhanced by the presence of alcohol, but it was unclear who would remember anything that was discussed by the following morning. Three drunk siblings began arguing over the best show from their childhood while one sober person quietly, yet forcefully, escorted them outside.

Chapter 2: Nebula

Morning rolled around, to the dismay of those who had spent the previous night drinking. Saturday was probably the worst morning for many people. It was next to impossible to get up and be active on one's free day. To be fair, however, most mornings were difficult in a college town. A simple glance at the city's coffee consumption statistics could prove that fact. Cafes were always packed, and the people that avoided those shops made their lucrative drinks at home. Some didn't rely on caffeine to get through their day, but no such person lived in a certain house.

Beams of light crept past a set of blinds and curtains to enter a moderately sized room. The wooden floor was almost spotless except for some random articles of clothing carelessly stripped off the previous night. A small TV on a large dark oak dresser gathered dust. Speakers alongside it improved the device's audio, and the universal remote was neatly placed in front. Across from the homemade entertainment center was a queen-sized bed where a tall man was sprawled out underneath the sheets. Next to the bed was a set of nightstands that held a lamp, an alarm clock, and an open book.

The rays of light extended their reach throughout the room as the sun continued to rise. Unfortunately for the sleeping man, he neglected to close his curtains before falling asleep. The full force of a solar assault hit him. The man tried to cover his face with his pillow, but it was too late. He was fully awake and couldn't return to his dreams. He groaned due to his lingering fatigue as his grim reality set in. Waking up exhausted was one of the worst feelings in the world.

Leo rose and stretched out his soreness from a full night of drinking and drunken sleeping. His once clean hair was now pressed into a flattened shape, and a stream of drool flowed along his cheek before he wiped it away. Leo moved to the edge of his bed and mentally prepared himself for the start of a new day. He rubbed his eyes as he stood, allowing his blanket to fall on the floor.

Oversized gym shorts rested on his hips. Without a shirt to cover his torso, Leo's body was revealed. His scars were plentiful. A set of three short ones resembling claw marks lined his lower ribs. A long thin scar arced from one shoulder to the other in a curved motion along his chest. Another sat near his neck and looked like the aftermath of a stab wound. Various other scars peppered his body, ranging in both size and shape.

Along with these scars was his Emblem. It was a pitch-black marking that followed Leo's spine. It flowed from the base of his neck to slightly above his rear end. Smaller perpendicular lines branched away from the main marking at each vertebra. It was a perfectly symmetrical structure that ended with a sharp point. One might even call it a work of art, depending on who was viewing it. Other Evolved envied such beautiful and easy-to-hide Emblems. Conversely, most of humanity still found the markings to be threatening and an eerie reminder of what monsters the Evolved could truly be.

At the end of Leo's marking, where the point should have been, was his ejected spine, once again ousted from its proper place. Its length was much shorter than its appearance from the previous night. At the time, it had moved with an intense purpose and acted swiftly. Now, the tail rested motionless on the bed at nearly half its previous length. Some additional dark matter had been created to sheathe the otherwise sharp edge on Leo's tailbone.

It was an interesting material for anyone who didn't fully understand it. The matter, ichor, was a hybrid between solid and liquid. Whatever form it took was up to the user, and it could be somewhat manipulated freely, based on the user's expertise. As a solid, ichor added durability to a structure and could withstand great amounts of force. Its liquid form granted mobility, flexibility, and extensibility.

Leo stood, and his spine was dragged off the bed and fell to the floor. He didn't seem bothered by it in the slightest. His morning routine continued without acknowledging the abnormality. Leo's tail subtly slid underneath the blanket on the floor. He flicked his appendage upward and flung the comforter into the air. He swiftly spun on his heels. Quick arms jetted from his sides to grab the free-floating blanket. Gentle hands guided the fabric to its proper place. A stretched tail reached across the bed to smooth out all the wrinkles that had formed.

This sort of utilization of one's Armament was to be expected. It was, after all, part of him. A part that was no different than his arms or legs. He frequently used it in a casual setting, like how he was now using it to pick up his discarded clothes. There was even a time when Leo would act like a monkey and hang from trees upside down. Of course, that took place long ago, when he was much younger and was still exploring his ability.

Leo snickered at the thought of his previous immature self as he stepped toward his dresser. He found an outfit for the day and quickly changed. His apparel from the previous night was tossed into the laundry basket. With its last job done, Leo's tail slowly returned to its original length before retracting into his body. His skin closed seamlessly, leaving no evidence that such a feat was even possible. The only thing that could confirm the Armament's presence was his Emblem, but even that was impossible to see, now that it was covered with a t-shirt. Leo slipped on his jeans and flicked his silver watch onto his wrist. He took a moment to wipe some of the dust off its face before uttering a silent prayer. Satisfied with his preparations, Leo left his room.

Several pictures lined the hallway. The photos depicted many key moments throughout the family's history and formed an easy-to-read timeline, starting from a collage of the children's first steps. Images of his late mother, Veronica, became less frequent as Leo walked down the hall. He never failed to smile as he walked past every frame, but the sudden absence of his father, Orion Sr., in the last few photos always hit the hardest. He grasped at his watch and kept his head down until he reached the kitchen at the end of the corridor.

A long granite counter extended across the entire kitchen, stopping just short of the adjacent living room and entryway. Above it was a series of cabinets filled with dishware. A newly bought microwave hung above the gas stove to replace one that had broken less than a month earlier. Close to the kitchen's corner was a recently installed stainless-steel sink with a drying rack next to it. Between the sink and stove was a three-fourths full coffee maker. A wooden board with "COFFEE" painted on it had several pegs to hold each resident's respective mug.

In the middle of the kitchen was a moderately sized table where Lyra sat alone. She was dressed in casual clothing, much like Leo, and was enjoying a delightful cup of coffee in peace. Steam rose from her mug as the scent of a fresh brew emanated throughout the room and spread into the hallway. The smell practically ran through the whole house, but no one would complain about that. The four siblings had a love for all things coffee-related. It was why they splurged to get custom-made mugs, the type that changed color in the presence of a warm liquid. Lyra's had turned black, revealing a constellation drawn in white. A harp was also faintly seen behind the heat-enhanced stars.

Lyra greeted her brother with a polite smile, and he returned it in kind before moving to prepare his mug. As he poured, his white cup slowly shifted into an eye-catching black. Stars suddenly appeared while lines connected each dot. Much like his sister, Leo had a mug with a constellation that matched his name. The image of a translucent lion faintly came into view when Leo's zodiac mug finished changing. He didn't prepare his drink to nearly the same degree as Lyra. Instead, Leo preferred to drink his coffee without additives, much to the disgust of his siblings.

The two drank in silence once Leo took a seat at the table. It was a peaceful moment where they could relax. The workweek was always busy and tedious. Weekends were usually the only time they had off, but even that wasn't a given. Thankfully, the family operated rather smoothly. No one complained about the workload or increase in household chores. They all understood that it was necessary and regretted taking it for granted. Leo fiddled with his watch and quietly thought to himself, *those two shouldn't have had to grow up so fast.*

"Carpe Diem? Did I miss something on the calendar? It's not like any birthdays are coming up," Leo said, trying his best to push away his thoughts. He gazed at his mug with quizzical eyes. He rubbed his fingers along its rim as regret set in. He knew what was coming up. It may not have been written on the calendar, but the four siblings had already agreed on what they would do on their extended weekend. Carpe Diem, a special coffee blend from a local shop, was made in preparation for important family events, and none was more critical than the coming date.

"Can we not start our three-day weekend off on the right foot?" Lyra said with a smile. She waved her hand like that act wasn't a big deal. It was a playful motion, but she dropped the facade almost immediately.

She looked down the hall Leo came from. Out of the four doors present, two were open. There were no lights nor stirring within the closed rooms, so it was safe to say the others were still asleep. Knowing this, Lyra felt comfortable enough to be honest with her twin brother.

She played with the golden feather pendant that hung from her neck while continuing her response, "Besides, hon, it'll be the anniversary soon. Might as well finish off the bag."

"*Our* three-day weekend? You got Monday off?" Leo's eyes widened for a moment. This was great news. Everyone would be together for the anniversary. They could visit the site as a family. Lyra initially told everyone that she couldn't make it because of a staffing problem at work, but it seemed like she finally got that problem solved. Even so, it was odd that she was telling him this now. Leo's eyes darted across the room and locked onto a whiteboard that hung between the kitchen and living room. He didn't feel like waiting for a response. His answer should have been up there.

A grid was made on the board using electrical tape, and the top row spanned all seven columns beneath it. Five dry-erase markers of different colors rested on the board's bottom tray. The current month and its corresponding dates were written in black, while the other four colors belonged to a respective sibling. Several details and events were outlined in those colors, and the current weekend had "THREE DAY WEEKEND!" written on the Saturday slot. Three different lines stretched across the following two days to show that three people were free all weekend. Leo found it odd that Lyra hadn't added her line into the bunch.

"Yeah. It took a bit of pleading and giving up the next holiday, but I got it off," Lyra said. She was still bitter about giving up a different day, but that was a trade she was willing to make. It was worth it so long as she was with her family. That was all that mattered. Lyra decided to elaborate further. "I didn't want to leave Cassie after she told us everything. It was probably the only reason I was given the day off."

"We should have expected something to happen around the anniversary. And, we definitely shouldn't have caved to her demands like we did," Leo said with downcast eyes. He felt like he was failing. The role he was desperately trying to fill continued to grow far beyond what Leo initially imagined. He thought relating to his siblings would be easy and that the finances would be the worst part. Unfortunately, that was far from the case. Orion was becoming more reclusive. Cassie's nightmares and trauma were resurfacing. If Lyra wasn't around, Leo would have undoubtedly crumbled under the pressure, and the same could be said about her with Leo.

"I don't know how dad did it. He had so much on his plate. From us to the Cele-" Lyra started to say but stopped immediately. She wanted to reassure her brother, but a noise behind her derailed her train of thought. Her mouth immediately shut and her eyes locked onto the hallway's doors. Footsteps and creaks reflected the fact that someone had woken up. A slight whirring sound and the flash of blue light beneath a door revealed the person's identity.

Orion's bedroom door opened to reveal his incredibly messy and dark room. The blue light from his computer monitors flickered as applications opened automatically. Orion was quick to leave his room. Exhaustion was painted on his face, and his eyes lacked the usual faint spark they had. Long sweatpants piled at his feet and dragged along the floor, which made him look shorter than he was. A black tank top covered his thin torso and did nothing to conceal his Emblem. The three lines were present on both arms, as always, but they were noticeably different. The lines were thorned and extended farther than normal. Not only that, they were receding to their normal size at a sluggish pace.

Orion scratched the back of his head as he yawned. His short footsteps had a slight wobble to them as if he was still drunk from the prior night. Hazy eyes followed the floor before scanning the kitchen. He gave an obligatory nod to his siblings before shuffling over to the coffee pot. Orion grabbed his mug from the rack and quickly filled it. Much like the other two, Orion's mug changed color with the presence of a warm liquid and formed a constellation. Stars displayed as the image of a hunter appeared through the lines. Keeping to his namesake, he held the Orion constellation in his hands.

"Big announcement? I'm guessing you got Monday off?" Orion asked immediately. He could recognize the brand of coffee that was prepared. Such a blend didn't come often, and Orion had gotten better at picking up small details like scent. His suspicions were confirmed the moment he took a sip. It was heavenly. Nostalgia filled his mind. He was brought back to the first day he ever had coffee. However, that moment in history didn't last long.

Leo stood up from his seat and prepared to work his magic on the stove. He brought out ingredients for a classic breakfast. The scent of coffee was quickly overwhelmed by the smell of cooking meat. Sizzling and popping could be heard as the oil fried what was in the pan. Eggs were tossed into the mix with a single hand, showing Leo's expertise in making this dish. He had made it many times. It was his go-to meal whenever he didn't know what else to cook.

Lyra also took initiative. She cleared the table and set out plates for everyone. Silverware and napkins were added with careful attention to detail. Lyra wanted everything to align perfectly, even if the tacky placemats from their late parents ruined the aesthetic. Those few mats clashed against the kitchen's overall design, but no one would ever suggest throwing them away. They would likely be stored in the garage with all of Veronic and Orion Sr.'s old stuff before it ever glimpsed the bottom of a trash can. The four could never get rid of anything that belonged to their parents.

Orion was also oddly nice. He decided to refill everyone's mugs with more coffee before brewing another pot. Leo almost stepped in to stop the usage of the expensive blend but refrained. It was just for today. Why not have fun and splurge? He would just mark it as another necessary expense.

With the three immersed in their tasks, no one heard the noises that came from the final closed room. A series of crashing and stumbling sounds fell on deaf ears before the bedroom door swung open. Cassie sauntered out of her room in a way that heavily contrasted the panicked noises from earlier. It was clear that she only woke up because of the conversations happening in the kitchen. She wanted to be a part of the ongoing discussion but didn't want to seem desperate. She also preferred to hide the fact that she had just fallen out of her bed. The attempt to appear composed and mature failed the moment someone noticed her tangled hair, baggy eyes, and exhausted demeanor. Her wrinkled NASA t-shirt and matching sweatpants complemented the "I'm already done with today and it hasn't even started" aura around Cassie. A portion of her Emblem could be seen from the back of her collar, but it was slowly retreating out of sight.

The spark in Cassie's eyes rekindled the instant she saw breakfast was ready. Everyone exchanged polite greetings before Cassie zeroed in on the coffee machine. She grabbed her mug from the wall and quickly prepared a drink. The pattern of mugs continued with Cassie's glass. White turned to black. Stars formed. A constellation was revealed, and the faint image of a woman looking into a handheld mirror was displayed. Cassie gulped the much-needed coffee from her Cassiopeia mug before sitting at the table. She sat next to Orion before dramatically placing her head next to her plate. Her groan echoed through the room as she made her current mood obvious. It was essentially the same image from the previous morning, but now she could be even more emphatic with her performance without risking public embarrassment.

"Looks like someone slept well. No nightmares?" Orion said with a sarcastic tone. He waited for the expected witty remark, but his sister wasn't in the right mindset to continue the friendly banter. A callous glare was all that he got. On anyone else, it might have been menacing. Cassie, on the other hand, just looked like a sick puppy to her older siblings.

"I feel like I'm dying," Cassie said before letting out another unnecessary groan. Her attention immediately shifted away from her brother and refocused on her suffering. She mumbled a few inaudible words in the way only a hungover person could. The others chuckled at their immature siblings. They knew the experience of youthful drinking and its painful aftermath. Cassie wasn't much younger than them, but she was still naive. She had yet to learn her limit and how to avoid going past it. Her older brother was always eager to point that out.

"And here I always thought you were the smart one," Leo said. He always gave the same condescending line every Saturday morning.

Even so, she wasn't making progress at bettering her self-control. The weeklong break between hangovers was enough to make her partially forget about the consequences of drinking, continuing the grueling cycle of self-destruction. Leo let out a soft chuckle. A few years before, he was exactly like his sister. They all were at one point in time. The only difference was that Cassie was taking much longer to control herself than anyone else had. She was still childish in that regard. Nothing was forcing her to mature as quickly as the others. Not that Orion was forced, either.

"On the bright side, there were no nightmares. Even with that scene yesterday. Didn't dream of anything, actually," Cassie said. What she told was a bold lie. Her dreams did reappear, just as they always did. It seemed as if there was nothing Cassie could do to remedy the situation, but complaining about it would do her no good. Quite the opposite. It would only shorten the time she'd have before being forced to see a doctor. That was why her hazy mind decided to lie. Unfortunately for her, the others didn't entertain the idea.

"Alright, sweetie. I'm putting my foot down. I'll call Aunt Emma and have her here by tomorrow," Lyra responded. The worry in her voice was obvious. Everyone had already agreed to get their aunt involved, but no one specified a time to contact her. This was likely Lyra's only chance to immediately schedule a meeting with their relative. Leo and Orion both nodded in agreement. They all wanted to fix the issue before it got any worse.

All except one person.

"No…" Cassie tried to say but pain singed her mind. She wanted to argue once again, but her energy left her. It was too early in the morning for a dispute. The actions she took the previous night still haunted her body. All signs pointed toward giving up the fight. Cassie yielded, allowing the conversation to change its course.

"Why not do an event in the meantime? It'll be a good way to open up the weekend. Plus, we're due for one, anyways," Leo said. He nodded to his brother.

Orion immediately pulled out his phone and prepared the random number generator. It was how the Lee family decided which of the five events would take place during their bi-weekly competition: a point-to-point race, a martial arts tournament, a marksmanship test with both rifles and pistols, a random team sport, or a random board game. The events were both simple and diverse, so everyone had an equal opportunity to win.

"Looks like we got a race," Orion responded. He showed his phone to everyone as if to prove what was decided. An unusual smile flashed across his face. He was oddly excited about the selected event. That glee quickly simmered down once he noticed the stern glares that Leo and Lyra gave him. Cassie kept her head firmly on the table, so she didn't see the silent exchange above her. All she could think about was the race she would undoubtedly win.

"Is that the best idea given recent events?" Leo asked.

"From what I've heard, the Primal was last spotted at the zone's southern border. Plus, there's always *someone* walking around at night. We should be fine." Orion said with an assuring voice.

"If you want to race that badly, Orion, then we can do it. Just give me a few minutes before the race to make a call. In the meantime, eat up." Lyra said.

She gave the final verdict to hold the family competition that night, but most of her concern was still present. Thankfully, the youngest sibling was done with her exaggerated suffering and ready to raise the room's mood. The mere mention of the night's race was enough to bring her spirit back. Her mobility was her pride and joy. It may have been dumb luck to have her favorite event when she was feeling down, but Cassie was not about to waste this opportunity.

Breakfast was served while the siblings continued their idle chatter. It had been months since the last race, so they needed to prepare. The course had to be mapped. The weather needed to be checked. Most importantly, a checkpoint system was to be implemented to prevent any type of cheating. The family also needed to consider any Primal and Enforcer activity, but most of that topic was pushed aside.

It was decided that the race would take place between their house and Fee's Oasis. Enforcers rarely patrolled that area, and the rogue Primal was located a good distance away. With both security risks managed, the siblings could set their sites on the race. The Dorado brothers were contacted and agreed to give the racers a bottle once they arrived. That specific IPA bottle was to be used as a token to show that the runner made it to their destination before turning back. The first person to make it home with a bottle would be crowned the winner and given the benefits that came with winning the bi-weekly competition.

The morning's meal quickly disappeared as excitement built within the kitchen. Once all the plates were practically licked clean, the group shifted to the adjacent living room. Cassie was the only one to stay behind. She had to follow one of the many house rules. It was now her job to clean the dishes because she didn't help prepare the meal. Orion and Lyra's actions were enough to justify them not helping with the end process. That meant that Cassie had to do her job alone, not that she cared. It was a basic rule that everyone followed, and her siblings were smart enough to avoid the consequences. Fortunately, she only had to clean a few items. It didn't take long before she was done.

A morning like this was rare. The four siblings were finally able to enjoy each other's company. Judging by the messy calendar on the wall, it was safe to say their schedules were hectic. They mostly only met for dinner and a short conversation. Smiles quietly appeared on each of them. It was a peaceful moment, one that blossomed in the middle of the storm that was their lives. Together, they laughed at the comedian on TV and forgot all about their worries.

⠲⠇⠆⠇⠀⠇⠆⠇⠒

Night came swiftly as the Lee family put their plans into motion. Leo rushed to the store and bought ingredients for the night's barbecue. Lyra contacted the Dorado brothers once again to reconfirm their cooperation and that the bottles were ready. Orion cleaned the grill and backyard before beginning his search for the best music to listen to. Finally, Cassie called two of her friends to watch the house and food while the race ensued.

The doorbell rang not long after she made the call. Cassie quickly moved to greet her guests. The first was the familiar barista, Sadie, from the previous day. Her azure eyes smiled when they saw Cassie. A short welcoming hug quickly took place before the two broke apart and entered the living room. Sadie gently placed her bag on an empty chair. As one would expect, she was no longer dressed in her semi-formal work attire. Instead, she wore a delightful yellow sundress that was almost as bright as her unwavering smile. Her thorned vine-like Emblem was plain to see. They twirled around her wrist before creeping up each arm, stopping halfway to dance around her elbows.

The second guest that followed closely behind Sadie was Audrey, dressing in a much warmer flannel shirt and dark jeans. Her expression was still locked in its usual uncaring state, but Cassie knew her friend was happy to be there. Much like the previous day, only the top of Audrey's Emblem could be seen. The circle's edge was slightly more visible, but that didn't provide any groundbreaking information. It was much like Cassie's or Leo's Emblems which could be hidden better than most others. Such a rarity was envied amongst the Evolved population because it resulted in less harassment from humans. That jealousy skyrocketed further when one learned how powerful each of their Armaments was.

"What's going on, Cassie? It's pretty rare to call us over on such short notice. Not that it's a problem if we hang out," Sadie said. She sat on the living room couch without a second thought. It was practically a reflex at this point. This was almost like her second home during high school.

The three friends had spent a lot of time together during their younger years, especially when Cassie moved from her old home. Sadie was well aware of the resurgence of her friend's nightmares, thanks to Audrey. At first, she was worried about the sudden call and short message, but her fears dissipated upon viewing Cassie.

"Thanks for coming. Same to you, Audrey. Our normal referee is busy tonight, so you two are lifesavers." Cassie said. She motioned her friends to the backyard before briskly walking to the kitchen. A tray of various meats and vegetables rested on the counter and was ready for the barbecue. She grabbed the tray and kicked the back door open to meet with the others.

"Good to know we're Plan B for your late-night shenanigans. I'm so glad we're missing date night for this," Audrey said, giving her usual dosage of sarcasm.

The three friends entered the fairly small backyard. Freshly cut grass was still wet from the rain that fell earlier in the day. A large grill sat next to the patio door, and the rest of the family was seated in portable lawn chairs. They perked up once the guests arrived.

"Glad to see you could make it. We can finally start the race," Orion said uncharacteristically. He was never this excited for the family's bi-weekly competitions, much less when the event was a race.

Even so, Orion was having a difficult time hiding his excitement. His glee could only be the result of some new trick that he believed would get him first place. That joy only grew once additional bets were made on top of the usual prize.

"Race? I didn't bring my running shoes," Sadie said. She was under the impression that tonight was a simple get-together. It was then that she noticed everyone was dressed in athletic apparel. All of them were warmed up and ready to sprint off into the distance.

"Not you, dope," Cassie said through a subtle chuckle. Sadie would have been an excellent competitor. Her agility would easily place her among the top contenders. She had always scored a medal during her time as a track and field athlete in high school. Her speed was only further enhanced once free-running became her passion. Unfortunately, this was a family affair. A separate competition would have to be held for friends at a later date.

Sadie and Audrey were given a brief explanation of their roles for the night. The two were responsible for cooking the items on the tray. Detailed instructions were written on the ideal cooking method and time for each vegetable and meat. After the two guests understood the basics of grilling, or at least feigned comprehension to send Leo away, the Lee family got ready for the race. Sadie took two drinks from the nearby cooler and sat with Audrey to watch the preparations.

Leo started by removing his shirt. He threw it onto an empty chair and showed off his back. The lengthy marking that covered his spine had been exposed, not that it surprised anyone present. They had all seen it before. The Emblem quickly grew and extended, starting from his neck and moving to his hips. Leo wasted no time ejecting his spine and whipping it around. His tail popped as it released some of the built tension before loosely swaying behind him. Each vertebra was still connected via ichor, which extended and contracted until the structure found its ideal length.

Lyra rolled up her sleeves to expose the web-like Emblem that covered her elbows. She gently rubbed her arms as if they were sore. The formation on each elbow branched outward. They became more erratic as they stretched further from their origin. Lyra raised her arms into the air before thrusting them down to the earth. Resting at her hips were two new bone structures. Both originated from the center of their respective webs. These Armaments heavily resembled side-handle batons and were coated in a surplus of ichor which had hardened to form a sharp serrated edge. Knowing her weapon's potential danger, Lyra bent her arms away from herself and the others.

Orion pulled his arms behind him to start a deep stretch. He let out a deep breath of relief as his back popped several times. His stretch ended when he quickly slammed his fists together. The markings along his arms rapidly expanded in an instant. The three lines branched and spread out before his skin tore. His radius and ulna bones burst through his flesh. The bones had separated and distanced themselves from their respective elbow, remaining attached to the wrist. A thin cord of ichor connected the two moving bones to form a 'D' with the grotesque materials. A third untethered and unnatural bone was found in the center of both arms. It raised out of his skin at a slight incline to sit atop his wrist. It was also sharpened much like an arrow. Orion relaxed his arms once the transformation was complete.

Cassie removed her college sweatshirt to reveal her massive Emblem. Two separate slits moved down her shoulder blades and ran parallel to her spine. Numerous branches and fracturing lines flowed out from the main two markings, encompassing most of her back. Cassie assumed a crouching position to ease her transformation. Her Emblem grew wildly, running amok on her body. A large amount of pressure built beneath her skin. She put her hands on the ground and kicked a leg back to stabilize herself. Summoning one's Armament was far from difficult, but Cassie wanted to add a bit of flair. The pressure that built within her released in a fraction of a second, and an enormous structure burst out of her back. The abhorrent wings that sprouted were an amalgamation of bones, blood, and ichor. They were far from beautiful, but visual appeal meant nothing to functionality.

"They're more fired up than usual. I guess a new bet was made?" Audrey asked. She turned to Sadie with a confused expression. She knew all about her friends' Armaments, so she was keenly aware that the performances were unnecessary. They'd all shown off their abilities before without the added fanfare. Audrey could only assume the siblings were trying to boost their egos and prepare for the race.

"That's what I heard," Sadie said. "Aside from the usual week of no chores, they also added unlimited access to one of the cars for that week."

Her explanation made perfect sense, and Audrey immediately understood what was at stake. With only two cars to share, the Lee family frequently argued over who deserved to drive. The Red Zone may have been congested, but driving was always better than walking. Plus, the weather was bound to get worse. Anyone in their right mind would choose the heated option rather than battling snowstorms to get to work or school. That was why free reign over a car was the grand prize. The week of no chores was simply the cherry on top.

"I guess this matters more than ever. Our poor little bird-brain is going to get her wings clipped soon," Audrey said with a coy smile. She recalled the Anti-Armament Law which had been officially passed recently. Its full effects and enforcement would take another few months, but that still meant Cassie would eventually be grounded. She would no longer be allowed to fly around the city and swiftly arrive at her destinations. Audrey almost felt bad for her friend, but that sympathy quickly dissolved once she realized the present issue didn't affect her. She rarely utilized her Armament in public. Even when she did, people didn't see her.

"Hey, start the countdown. I want to eat at some point tonight," Leo said. He could practically feel his stomach rumbling. The race may not have been long, but he didn't want to waste any more time than was necessary. If the idle conversations delayed the race any longer, his hunger would hinder his performance. The others felt the same but didn't voice their opinions.

"On it," Sadie said with glee. She could see why the others were in a hurry even if she wasn't. She and Audrey had already eaten dinner, so they had no reason to rush. Sadie stood from her seat and began the typical starting banter. The four runners assumed proper stances at the edge of the patio. Cassie's wings readied. Leo's tail whipped around. Orion's arm-bows prepared to fire. Lyra's batons became more serrated and slightly curved near the end.

With a single shout from Sadie and a sarcastic cheer from Audrey, the race began.

Cassie was off to an early lead, as per usual. Her wings always gave her a significant boost at the start of every race. The gust of wind that blew behind her also hindered her siblings. Cassie immediately extended her wings to catch the wind beneath them. She easily flew over the fence and neighboring houses. Meanwhile, her three siblings were forced to use more human methods to bypass the first set of obstacles.

It wasn't long before the group exited the residential area and found themselves in the dense city. The Red Zone's buildings were frequently compressed or incomplete. This poor planning and lack of budget left the zone a nightmare to navigate for any non-native. Cassie snickered as she glided over the streets and alleys that everyone else had to run through. Her confidence continued to build, eventually becoming arrogant. She truly thought that no one could touch her from way up high. A curious glance behind her was supposed to further bolster her pride, but it crushed her ego instead.

The sight before her was unlike anything she had ever dreamed of.

Orion was right behind her. He was flying through the air at a blinding speed. His figure zoomed by Cassie's field of vision before she could completely register what she had witnessed. Her head snapped forward to reconfirm what was once impossible. Orion was airborne, but he wasn't flying like Cassie. He was swinging. A long cord of ichor stretched out of his wrist where the third bone once rested. The other end of the line was embedded into a nearby building and acted as an anchor for Orion's feat of dexterity. Meanwhile, his other arm hung loosely behind him as it prepared its next arrow.

What the hell?! Cassie thought, *How is he in the air?!* Tension built within her as she analyzed the obvious answer. Orion could only ever shoot arrows with his arm-bows. Tethering ichor to them should have been impossible. His Armament focused primarily on ranged attacks and accuracy. It was why he was classified as a ranged-type Evolved rather than a mobile or hybrid like Cassie or Leo.

It was then that more of Orion's new trick was revealed. With a flick of his wrist, the line of ichor retracted at an alarming speed. The third bone that was stuck in the building dislodged itself and zipped back to its owner. Orion then twisted his body and fired his next shot. It all started to make sense. His speed came from the constant swinging and slingshot-like retraction. That same retraction also meant that he wasn't wasting ichor, so Orion didn't have to expend energy to create more. It was an ingenious way to travel, which is why it bothered Cassie to no end.

Since when could he make rope shots?! Cassie's bewildered thoughts continued, *And why is he so good with them?!* Cassie was astonished. Her altitude dropped as she watched her brother pull ahead. Orion may have been able to change the general structure of his arrows, but he could never affix ichor to them. Something must have happened between now and the previous race that allowed him to mutate. Intensive training wasn't something Orion would do willingly, so this must have been the result of pure luck. That was how most Evolved mutations were, though they were too rare to confirm that fact. Cassie couldn't contain her thoughts. She tried to identify a point in time when Orion acted differently or hid more than he usually did.

"You're losing your edge, Cassie," Leo said from above. His sister immediately snapped out of her thoughts. He decided to tease his bewildered sister by landing on her back. Cassie flailed from the sudden increase in weight but soon proved that she was strong enough to carry others. It wasn't a revolutionary discovery by any means, but Cassie was also unfamiliar with catching people out of the air. Leo knew his ride was limited. His sister had plenty of ways to kick him off once she stabilized herself, so he took initiative and hopped off. He pushed Cassie down to propel himself up and utilized his tail to swing in the same way Orion did.

Cassie was left dumbstruck. She was always the first to finish the family races. Her mobility was her best quality. So, how did her brothers manage to improve this quickly and without her notice? It had only been a few months since their last race. Cassie hung her head low. She turned herself to auto-pilot mode to think for a moment. Answers wouldn't come from thin air. She would simply have to get them once the race was over. In the meantime, she needed to win back her honor as a mobile-type Evolved. Cassie flapped her wings to increase her speed and altitude. Obviously, she needed a better plan to beat her brothers than simply fly over everything, but that was the best idea she had so far. It was then that she noticed a third anomaly.

Lyra was running in the alley beneath her flying siblings. Her movements were precise and calculated. The tall fences and other large obstacles posed no threat to her. Lyra turned and twisted through routes that should have been unknown to her. She even used her curved batons to hook her obstacle, giving her better leverage when vaulting over the tallest of barriers. Of course, most of this route was lost on Cassie. She had no reason to know the intricate map of back alleys one could take. She also flew above everything, so memorizing her sister's route was pointless.

No way, Cassie thought. She flapped her wings. The shock of Orion's new trick left her body as she realized her current position in the race. Cassie kept a close eye on her sister as she rapidly increased her speed. She refused to come in last place. Lyra's route never interested her, but Cassie was focusing on it more than ever. Her massive wings continued to flap. She needed to increase her altitude. She needed to fly faster. Those simple commands repeated in her mind several times while she kept her focus locked on the ground. Unfortunately, Cassie had never practiced the art of tracking a target while navigating a congested cityscape.

She wasn't ready for Lyra to suddenly make a sharp turn.

Wha-?! Cassie tried to think, but her mind couldn't keep up. She stared at the ground for too long. She never noticed how high she was. She didn't take into account that others may be present. Worst of all, she failed to see the person standing on a nearby rooftop.

Suddenly, a sharp pain assaulted her. The sound of a gunshot rang throughout the night. Cassie couldn't believe what had happened. Her wings had been clipped. They were torn via a well-aimed shot from a man clad in violet armor, an Enforcer. His gun was the same dark shade as the rest of his gear. All of it was made from the same material, and its sole purpose was for eliminating Evolved. This Anti-Evolved, or AE for short, was expensive to make, so only Enforcers and high-ranking officials were allowed to utilize it.

Cassie skipped off the rooftops like a stone on water. She had no way of slowing herself. Her wings were inoperable. They cried in pain, but Cassie couldn't help them. All she could do was flail as she tumbled across a flat rooftop and skidded against its asphalt. She felt it rub away her skin as friction slowed her. It would have been best to stay on a roof so that she could jump off it and gain flight speed from the descent, but fate was cruel. Cassie slid off the roof and plummeted to the earth. She twisted her body and used her wings to protect her.

She landed with an audible thud and a sickening crunch. She let out a cry of pain as she rolled on the ground. Her heavy breathing showed how much her body ached. Every movement took a considerable amount of energy. The ends of her limbs grew cold. Her wings were useless and unresponsive. Cassie knew she needed to flee. She yelped as she rose to her feet and shuffled along the alley. She used a nearby building for support as she pushed herself forward. There had to be somebody to help. Anybody. Someone that could pull her from this nightmare. Unfortunately, she was given the opposite.

Another brutal shot clipped her back. Her wings took the brunt of the blow, but some of the excess AE material seeped into her flesh. Cassie no longer questioned what firearm was being used. It was a shotgun. One that fired many AE pellets. The very same type that could tear through any normal Evolved's defenses. One would have to be blessed as an armored-type or be extremely lucky to survive multiple shots. Cassie knew she was on borrowed time. As a last-ditch effort, she fell to the ground and feigned her own death.

Don't move, Cassie thought to herself. She could hear the Enforcer's footsteps grow closer. Thankfully, the remnants of her wings hid some of Cassie's visible breathing. She continued to take shallow breaths before stopping completely. The Enforcer had reached her. He waited for a few seconds but never confirmed if his target was dead. Instead, he decided to enjoy his achievement and boast to anyone that would listen.

"Kilo, it's Romeo. I got one. A mobile-type with wings. Young. Female," Enforcer Romeo said to his partner via radio. He circled Cassie several times. He examined her face to guess her age. A cruel foot pressed against her to see if she would react. Of course, Cassie wouldn't budge. She was too afraid. She would be killed the moment Romeo realized she was alive. That was confirmed by what he said next.

"Look, I don't care what you tell Alpha in the report. The damned Evolved was flying around in the middle of the night. If she ain't a Fallen or Primal, then she's breaking curfew and the new Anti-Armament law."

The silence was deafening as Romeo waited for a response from his partner.

"Yeah. Just make sure to take your time with the paperwork, so we can enjoy hunting before open season officially begins."

Romeo continued his casual conversation while Cassie's mind went into a frenzy. She was panicking. None of her siblings could withstand a sneak attack from an Enforcer. They didn't have the luxury of large protective wings to take the brunt of the blow. They'd all be gravely wounded from the first shot, if not killed outright. Cassie's fear exploded. She wouldn't be able to live with herself if another person she loved died.

It almost drove her to action, but Romeo stopped her when he began speaking to her, "Filthy Evolved. You don't deserve the wings of an angel. You deserve to be sent back to the pit of hell you crawled-"

A rustle of trash cans stopped Romeo mid-speech. He turned to face the source of the sound. His weapon was readied. He aimed it at the new figure. All of which happened outside of Cassie's field of view. She could only hear Romeo's shaking breath as he saw whatever beast entered the fray. Yes, beast. That was what she assumed it was. It gnarled and growled. Its breathing was arrhythmic and audibly disturbing. There was no need to visibly confirm what it was. Cassie knew this was a Primal. One that crawled out of her nightmares and into the real world. She felt her muscles tense. A new type of fear set in her. Her mind wanted to flee, but her body refused to move.

"Halt. I am Enforcer Romeo. If you come any closer I'll-" Romeo started to say but stopped abruptly.

The two individuals suddenly clashed when the Primal rammed into the Enforcer. Romeo let out a grunt. The air was forced out of his lungs. He quickly pulled the trigger. A shot rang out, but it only grazed its target. Not wasting the opportunity, the monster continued its rush. It pushed Romeo into the nearby building, slightly coming into Cassie's view. She could see the Primal utilize its large horns to deal considerable damage. The Enforcer tried to resist, but he dropped his weapon during the unorthodox assault.

The struggle continued for what felt like an eternity. Cassie desperately attempted to maintain her facade. Romeo could feel his innards being skewered with each additional thrust from the beast. Splatters of blood fell on Cassie as the Primal continually pistoned its horns into Romeo's stomach. After a minute of its non-stop assault, the beast stepped back. The Enforcer's lifeless body dropped to the ground next to Cassie, spilling a pool of blood that stained her clothes. She couldn't see what happened next, but it wasn't hard to assume the scenario. That was when it got much worse.

I'm going to die, Cassie thought, feeling sick to her stomach. She could sense the Primal behind her. Its eyes watched her with a piercing glare. It didn't need to confirm if she was alive. A small-minded monster would either kill her again or simply eat her alive. The choice was up to Cassie on what she would do: whether she kept up the charade or sprinted into the distance. Primals weren't invincible. It would take a few confident Evolved, but they'd be able to slay the beast. Primals avoided densely populated areas for that very reason. This one must have been new and didn't know where it was. If that was the case, it might still chase Cassie into the Red Zone's main streets.

The horrifying sound of a lifeless body hitting the ground echoed in her head. It compounded with the sensation of Romeo's blood coating her side. Chills went down her spine as she imagined her corpse being added to the pile. That couldn't happen. There had to be a way out. The moment she got the chance, Cassie would sprint out of the alleys and onto the streets. From there, others would surely help her. It wasn't a solid plan, but it was the best one she could think of. Staying only guaranteed her death when the Primal got to her. The steps grew closer. Cassie could feel her body become a frozen figure. She couldn't move. All that raced was her mind.

Then, the Primal sank its teeth into its victim.

⁖⠇⠒⠇⠇⁖⁙

I'mgonnadie, I'mgonnadie, I'mgonnadie, Cassie's thoughts looped. Her frigid body kept her locked in place, frozen in fear. It was enough for the Primal to ignore her. Or rather, the monster preferred to dine on fresh meals. It was more than willing to analyze Cassie and see if she was worth devouring after it was done with the man. The Primal avoided most of Enforcer Romeo's armor. After all, it was AE equipment. Ingesting the gear was the quickest way to kill one's self.

The sound of chewing was practically next to Cassie's ear. She could hear every bone snap. The Enforcer's flesh was torn from his body with an audible ripping sound. Droplets of blood splashed on the ground. What made it all worse was imagining the origin of each sound and how they'd soon apply to her. The poor girl would flail in a panic if she could, but she didn't want to alert the Primal. No, someone else wanted to be the one to incur the Primal's wrath.

"Get the hell away from her!" A deep voice called out. Before the Primal could react, a man crushed it beneath his heels when he fell from the sky. He immediately jumped toward Cassie, scooped her off the ground, and ran with her in his arms. He kept glancing down to see if she was alright, but it was hard for Cassie to tell where he was looking due to the mask he wore. It was a large blue mask with golden gears affixed to it, which ticked to wind the large mainspring over his right eye. The cogs would eventually halt to release the spring's tension before resuming the never-ending cycle.

"T-Tartarus?!" Cassie blurted. She may have been injured, but she wasn't in a state where she wouldn't recognize the man. He was one of the battalion commanders from the Night of A Thousand Blades. To be specific, he was the Assault Battalion Commander. His strength was unquestionable as was his leadership. Cassie wanted to ask all sorts of questions but now wasn't the time. The unimaginable duo had to survive their encounter with the Primal.

"I was following that Enforcer to see what he was up to. Never imagined it'd bring me to you." Tartarus said. Though he was dressed in a full cobalt suit, he had no issue running at full speed. Quite the opposite. He preferred this attire when in combat. It gave him a sense of nostalgia for his glory days. Tartarus glanced at Cassie's wings. They were still tattered and injured. He clicked his teeth and spoke, "Recall your wings, and take a vial of Nectar out of my chest pocket."

Cassie did as she was told. The destroyed remnants of her wings seeped back into her body, though not without a great deal of pain. She still felt them within her. It would take time, but they would be repaired naturally. That was where the Nectar came in. Cassie frantically pressed against her savior's chest to find the pocket before plunging her hand into it. There were several vials of medicine that would help her, but she chose not to be stingy. Tartarus ordered her to grab one, and he might need the others for himself or the next person that needed saving. She took the vial and quickly ingested the bitter liquid.

"How long until you can fly?" Tartarus asked. It was a complicated question. Evolved regeneration was swift, but it wasn't immediate. Cassie would need time before she could return to her pristine self. The Nectar would help expedite the process but at a cost. Other factors such as the scope of the injury, her natural regeneration speed, and the AE matter that wounded her also had to be taken into account. An exact answer was impossible to give. It could be hours or even days before Cassie was back to normal. That, however, wasn't what Tartarus asked.

"Ten to twenty minutes. If I focus, I can stitch my wings enough to fly for a bit. Carrying both of us will suck, but I can-" Cassie tried to say before she felt the arms that held her move. Her explanation was interrupted when Tartarus had heard enough. He thrust his leg out to stop his sprint. His body twisted as he threw Cassie into an adjacent alleyway, out of the Primal's line of sight.

"I'll buy you as much time as I can! Get home as fast as you can! That's an order!" Tartarus shouted.

He spread out his arms to get the Primal's attention. Ichor poured from his wrists before solidifying and crystallizing into jagged claws. The structure nearly tripled the size of his regular hands and was more than capable of cutting through any material. This was a sight that any Evolved would be honored to see. The commander of the Assault Battalion was preparing for an intense fight. What Evolved in their right mind wouldn't get goosebumps from watching their hero fight against evil incarnate?

Against him stood the monster that terrified Cassie. It was nothing like the nightmares of her mother. The Primal's horns were overgrown and serrated. Jagged ichor shards replaced its teeth. Whoever the beast once was, they lacked defining features from their old life. They were disgustingly thin to the point of being nothing but bones, and ichor blotched their skin. One of their eyes was missing while its counterpart was sunken and lifeless.

"Go, Cassiopeia! I won't tell you again!" Tartarus said before the fight ensued.

The Primal immediately leapt into action. It swept Tartarus off his feet with a clean strike from its horns and carried him out of sight. The beast suddenly stopped to throw its enemy off. Tartarus stumbled back before recollecting himself. He rubbed his stomach to confirm that the wound wasn't fatal.

The Primal's head shook as its arm twitched. The ichor-covered limb dropped to the ground and extended to an abhorrent length. Spikes burst from its flesh. Another mutation. The Primal must have deemed Tartarus to be a significant threat if it was modulating its body. The beast whipped its elongated arm around for an overhead attack, but Tartarus dodged at the last second. He stomped on the stretched limb and slashed through it with his claws. The Primal roared as it recoiled, and Tartarus charged forward to retaliate.

Meanwhile, Cassie was running for her life. She never thought she could run so fast. Once the Primal was out of her sight, it was like the frost around her had vanished. The fear disappeared in an instant. Cassie wasn't sure if it was because she trusted Tartarus or because she knew she could get away, but those questions could be answered at a later time. Her sole objective was to flee. She almost tripped over herself several times during her panicked sprint. Cassie didn't know if the Primal had mutated an Armament for tracking, but anything was possible at this point. She needed to get as much distance between her and them as possible.

The sound of fighting and roaring grew quieter with each step. It wasn't clear who was winning, but both were struggling to completely win over the other. That single fact was terrifying to Cassie. Tartarus was the Assault Battalion Commander. He was known for his incredible strength and battle prowess. If he couldn't beat the Primal, who could? It was true that he was far past his prime, but that shouldn't have dulled him to the point of losing against a mindless beast. At least, that was what Cassie hoped.

As the dust settled and time passed, she eventually summoned her wings. They ached in pain with every motion. Cassie almost considered staying on the ground but convinced herself out of that thought. She needed to fly away before anything else happened. Her ichor-patched wings launched her several feet into the air. Cassie frantically flapped to keep herself afloat. It was much like when she first learned to fly. Her movements were chaotic, and she bounced off the nearby buildings a few times. Thankfully, nothing serious happened during her ascent. There were no more Enforcers. No other Primals found themselves in the area. Even the lack of masked people willing to help put Cassie's mind at ease. She was exhausted and needed to return home.

Wow, Cassie thought to herself. She reflected on everything that had happened. How she was shot out of the sky. How a Primal managed to easily slay an Enforcer equipped to combat Evolved of all types. How a literal living legend stepped into the fray to save her. And, most impressive of all, how she somehow managed to survive all of that. There was a lot to think about, but only one thought was on Cassie's mind at the moment. *I can't believe I just met Tartarus! Ah! The others are going to be so jealous! Well...if we all live, that is...*

She worried about accidentally guiding the Primal back to her home. The thought of inadvertently killing her family by allowing a monster to follow her was mortifying. Cassie considered flying in an unorthodox path but immediately dismissed the idea. Her wings weren't in a condition to freely fly. At this point, they were glorified beams to adjust the speed at which she hit the ground. She was more likely to crash into her backyard than anything else.

Wait, Cassie continued her train of thought, *how did he know my name?* It was one of many questions that she had about the night, but it was also one of the most interesting ones. Obviously, Cassie wasn't her real name. It was a shortened version so that people had an easier time talking to her. Most assumed the nickname was short for Cassandra, but her full name was Cassiopeia Lee. She was named after a constellation much like her siblings, though their names sounded normal compared to hers. She was rarely called by her real name, so the encounter was off-putting. If Tartarus had known her, he would have called her Cassie. His slip-up showed that he was familiar with her but was not on close terms with her, like an estranged uncle of sorts.

Cassie followed this web of ideas and coincidences until a presence behind her snapped her back into reality. It was a sort of looming figure that rose above the gliding girl. She wanted to fly faster but that would have torn her wings apart. At this point, all she could hope was the people in her neighborhood would hear the commotion and help her. She clenched her fist and turned to see the threat that was upon her.

It was Orion.

He was tumbling through the air behind his sister. The residential area lacked tall buildings, except for a few apartment complexes. This left Orion with nothing to swing from nor a safe way to slow his descent. He was stranded high in the air with little to no options. The final shot whipped through the night sky as it returned to Orion's wrist, not that it could offer much help. Trees and low buildings littered the ground and taunted him. His eyes darted around the expansive area for an answer, but his choices were finite. He was left to the whims of fate.

That fate was to crash into his sister. Both had limited evasive maneuvers. One was out of exhaustion and wounds from battle. The other was out of ignorance. These circumstances led to a marvelous collision. Orion managed to land directly on Cassie's back, knocking the air out of her lungs. Her sore wings failed to support the sudden additional weight. They automatically retracted back into her body. Within seconds, the two siblings were plummeting to the earth. A tree and bush tried to cushion the landing but couldn't completely reduce the damage dealt. They flipped, flailed, and screamed before miraculously landing in their backyard. Audrey and Sadie watched the entire event unfold, and Audrey made sure to take several photos.

"Sorry. I'm still getting used to traveling in the residential area," Orion said as he rose from the ground. Leaves and sticks had latched onto him during the fall. A noticeable amount of dirt and grass sullied his clothes. He was still out of breath from running and swinging through the race. The bottle that he had received from Fee's Oasis was shattered, but Orion was mostly fine. His main concern was about his sister's reaction to his new trick.

Orion turned to ask the pressing question. "So, what'd you think? Pretty nifty, right?"

Cassie didn't respond. Her clothes were disheveled and damaged more than any accident could cause. Moderate bruising was found along her arms. Open wounds peppered her back where her wings failed to protect her, and she was coated in a considerable amount of blood. Her wings had retracted, which was odd. Cassie should have used them to soften her landing but chose not to. The unexplainable details caused a barrage of countless questions to assail the others.

"Cassie?" Orion called out to his sister. A gut-wrenching feeling settled in his stomach. Something extremely horrible must have happened, and he didn't know how to react. Cassie had never been in a state like this before. No one had. They avoided fights and rarely made mistakes that resulted in such injuries. Orion's vision focused on his sister. Everything around her faded into the background. His hands trembled as he thought, *What do I do? What's the right course of action? I have to help her but... Do I worry about whatever did this? What could have even gotten her from so high? Dammit! I don't have time!*

"Guys! Are you alright?! The alley on the way back was all torn up like-" Leo started to say as he strolled over the fence. He was worried about the others. His returning path brought him to the scene where Cassie fell. Of course, he wasn't aware of her experience. All he saw was the aftermath. He discovered Enforcer Romeo's corpse. He noticed how it was disfigured and partially eaten. He ran along the alley that had been destroyed from some sort of battle between Evolved. All evidence pointed toward it being the work of a Primal. Leo rushed home as quickly as he could and found Cassie in her broken and battered state.

"I crashed into her mid-flight, but I don't know where the rest of the damage came from," Orion said with a shaking voice.

Audrey and Sadie both confirmed what they saw. No one could explain what had happened to Cassie, but it wasn't hard to guess what caused her injuries. Leo ran over to his sister and analyzed her wounds. Unlike Orion, he was able to keep his composure and assess the situation properly.

"Sadie, get the Nectar from our first aid kit!" Leo shouted at his guest.

Sadie sprinted into the building to do as she was told.

Cassie's obvious external wounds were worrying, and there was no way to tell what was wrong internally. The excessive amount of blood also needed to be addressed. Of course, they didn't know most of it was from Enforcer Romeo. Cassie was exhausted from her injuries and was slowly fading out of consciousness. Evolved could automatically heal their wounds using their ichor, but its generation took a significant amount of time and energy. Cassie had lost most of hers when she patched her wings and partially restored her back. That was why Leo wanted to urgently give her Nectar.

Fortunately, Sadie was swift with her acquisition and emerged from the house. The square bottle she carried was half empty and contained a crimson liquid, Nectar. A silver label covered the bottle's midsection with its name written in bold letters. Under the title was the image of an angel filling a pitcher from a waterfall. The item looked incredibly ornate. One could easily mistake it for an expensive beverage, but that was far from the case. Nectar was a medicine designed specifically for Evolved.

This popular medicine was a mainstay in all Evolved first aid kits due to its universal applications. It was able to increase one's natural production of ichor by acting as an extremely efficient fuel source. That generated ichor was then used to heal and rejuvenate the Evolved. The process, however, only sped up recovery time, so a wave of exhaustion always hit the user once the medicine was out of their system. This side effect had yet to be circumvented due to the medicine's relatively recent release. Other versions of the drink existed because the recipe was easy to find and alter, but they weren't fully tested nor mass-produced.

Leo took the bottle from his friend and popped off the top. He fed its contents to Cassie and hoped for the best. Contrary to its name, Nectar was an incredibly bitter drink. Cassie recoiled from the taste, as most would. The small dose from earlier was nothing compared to this. She was repulsed by the overwhelming flavor but drank it anyway. Her retracted wings felt revitalized. The wounds on her back closed at a sluggish pace. Even the bruises that peppered her body were fading. Cassie used what little strength she could muster to push away the bottle.

"Don't fight me on this. Just drink the damned Nectar. You can explain what happened in the morning," Leo said. He could see the many things that were lulling his sister to sleep. The Nectar was taking its toll on her body. The stress of whatever situation she was just in left her weary. Then, there was the adrenaline that kept her moving until she got home. Now that she was safe, Cassie's body was quick to shut down and recover. Leo rubbed his silver watch. He felt pathetic. It was his idea to hold the event today, and the results were clear. He had inadvertently put his family, the people he was entrusted to protect, in danger. No one blamed him, yet he still felt guilty.

A hand reached out and grabbed Leo's shoulder to pull him back into reality. It was Lyra. She was the last one to arrive home and see the scene. She calmly motioned her head to the house and guided her brother to the patio. Leo followed her without a word, taking Cassie in his arms and carrying her with care. He quietly made his way to her room and rested his sister on her bed.

Meanwhile, Lyra stayed with the others. She maintained her calm and collected facade, but her mind was panicking. There was no way to assure everyone or to keep them from acting out. She shot a glance at Orion to send him into the house. She suggested that Sadie and Audrey stay the night and make use of her room. They happily obliged and entered the home, unwilling to leave at a time like this. Finally alone, Lyra pulled out her phone. She slowly dialed a phone number before deleting it. This wasn't the time to bother *him*. Instead, she called someone else.

Chapter 3: Fusion

The following morning, sun rays seeped into a cluttered room. They highlighted the numerous articles of clothing and random papers that peppered the floor. Most of the documents and notes were centered around a disorganized desk that its owner neglected to clean. Various reports, essays, and books sat alongside a slim laptop computer. They had been slightly shifted to make room for a small cup of coffee.

Resting in the equally messy bed was Cassie. She clung to her large pillow and kicked off her blanket at some point in the night. Her wounds were gone but their effects still lingered. The young Evolved had yet to recover all of her ichor, leaving her in a deep sleep. Not even the risen sun was enough to wake her. She continued to slumber as if nothing was wrong and ignored her silent guest.

A quiet middle-aged woman sat at the cluttered desk. Her posture was exemplary despite the relaxed chair she sat in. Her curious emerald eyes stared at a nearby bookshelf that housed a variety of novels. Six circle markings prominently stood out against her almond skin. They rested along her brow and around her eyes to form a symmetrical pattern. The Emblem was simple yet intriguing, though a large portion of it was covered with her dark brown hair. It led most people to question what her Armament was and how the two were related.

The woman sat in silence while enjoying her drink until an alarm suddenly blared. Cassie had neglected to turn it off once the weekend began. It was a mistake she made quite often and constantly forced her to start the day in a foul mood. Luckily, her guest was kind enough to silence the noise immediately. The woman's hand jetted toward the sound's source. A line of ichor ejected from her palm and stuck to the digital clock across the room. The string then retracted back into her body, bringing the chirping alarm with it. She clasped it with a firm grip and switched it off.

Unfortunately, the swift response didn't save Cassie from waking up. Her heavy eyes sluggishly opened. Her head swiveled to view the room. Once she spotted the woman at her desk, Cassie's heart skipped a beat. She instinctively hugged her pillow and shrunk into the corner, too startled to summon her wings and utilize them as a shield. The moment was intense, but the tension immediately subsided once she recognized her guest.

"Why do you have to be so quiet, Aunt Emma?! You seriously don't need to use those things all the time," Cassie said before catching herself.

She pinched the bridge of her nose. Regret immediately set in. Her outburst was uncalled for. It was common knowledge not to criticize another person's Armament, especially those of older generations. Cassie was simply fed up with the scares that resulted from her aunt's constant usage of her extraordinary ability. Emma was always training her skills by using her Armament at any available instance. She also had a habit of leaving small webs of ichor whenever she got distracted or wanted to pass time.

"Those things? Ridiculous. They are threads of ichor. They aid in my mobility and stealth. You should know that," Emma said in a robotic tone. Her interesting speech pattern was yet another reason Cassie felt uneasy around her. Emma rarely expressed emotion, and her voice matched her permanently neutral demeanor. In general, she was off-putting. Even close relatives and friends couldn't get a good read on her. Emma, of course, knew this but never bothered to change. It was how she was created. It was how the good doctors desired her, so it was how she wished to remain. She continued talking to her niece. "You seem much better. How are you feeling?"

"Good, but I'm still pretty tired. Thanks for watching over me. I'm sorry for all the trouble," Cassie said with a slight bow. Now that she recovered from the initial shock, she couldn't help but act a bit more formally around her aunt.

It was odd. The two were family. There was no need for such formalities, but something about Emma told Cassie to be on her best behavior. Cassie tossed her pillow aside and rose to her feet. She noticed that her clothes had been changed at some point in the night. Her sullied running attire was replaced with her typical pajamas. She gave a silent thanks to whoever had the foresight to prevent her bed from soaking that filth.

"Report to your siblings," Emma said before gesturing to the door.

Her expression didn't change as she stared at her niece, but Cassie could tell she wanted to say more. A barrage of questions was waiting to be answered. The moment Cassie left her room would be when it all kicked off. She took a deep breath and braced for the worst. She walked past her aunt and nudged open the door.

Five sets of ears perked up at the sound of a door creaking. The three remaining siblings stood in the kitchen. Orion paced by the coffee maker as it brewed Cassie's favorite drink, butter pecan coffee. Leo worked his magic on the stove, flipping pancakes like an expert. Lyra scanned through the available songs on her phone before landing on the perfect playlist. Meanwhile, the two guests patiently sat in the living room. Sadie flipped through channels on the TV to find a good show, and Audrey looked for funny posts on social media. Almost everything they did was geared toward making Cassie as comfortable as possible. From breakfast to the genre of music playing, all her favorite things were on display. The group reflexively tensed once the woman of the hour walked in.

They tried their best to act casually, but the attempt backfired. Orion panicked and pretended to drink out of an empty mug. Leo lost focus mid-flip and made a small mess while making the final pancake. Lyra started to dial random numbers on her phone. Sadie accidentally muted the TV and struggled to find a way to rectify the issue. Audrey was the only person to maintain their composure, but that was because she got distracted by a cat video.

Cassie tried to rub the exhaustion out of her eyes as she approached the table. She, once again, had slight bags under her eyes and was visibly pale. Her heavy footsteps caused the floor to creak. She pulled out one of the many chairs and made herself comfortable. Her usual mug was lovingly prepared ahead of time and readily sat on the table. Emma silently followed her niece like a looming ghost. She took a seat at the head of the table where she always sat when she visited.

"You guys are bad at acting casual," Cassie said with a low voice. She was the first to break the awkward silence which caused everyone to flinch.

They thought it would take significant effort to get her to open up. It dawned on the five how ridiculous they were behaving. Infectious smiles immediately spread throughout the room. They stopped their various actions and sat around the kitchen table. Plates were set, extra chairs were added, and breakfast was served.

"Guilty as charged," Leo said with a sigh. His effort to ease the tension in the room only added attention to it. They would have preferred to start the barrage of questions, but uneasiness still lingered. It didn't feel right. Cassie needed time to breathe and reflect.

"They were an inconvenience. Nothing but panic," Emma said as she ate. She recalled how the previous night went from her perspective. She had closed her shop and was ready to enjoy a peaceful evening alone when her niece, Lyra, called for help. Something had gone wrong, and Lyra didn't trust herself to manage everything without additional assistance. Nectar was administered, but it didn't hurt to contact another medical professional. Emma arrived on the scene within minutes and promptly kicked everyone out of Cassie's room.

"You scared us pretty bad," Orion said with a low voice. He still felt awful about his actions. He should have handled it better.

That same type of guilt hung over everyone. Leo felt bad about suggesting the race. Lyra believed she failed by not clearing the racecourse beforehand. Sadie thought she was too slow to retrieve the Nectar. Only one person didn't feel a weight on their shoulders, and she was also coarse enough to push the conversation along.

"So, what made you fall out of the sky? Get shot down?" Audrey asked. She cocked her head to the side and gave a sly grin. It was rather rude, but no one expected anything more from her. That was just how she was. Leo had half a mind to tell her off but refrained. He didn't want to miss the chance of progressing the discussion.

"Actually, I did. Some Enforcer did it. I think the guy's name was Romeo," Cassie said. She tried to remember everything that had happened. Most of it was a blur. It was a period of non-stop action with each step adding more questions to the pile. Cassie would have preferred to give a concise answer, but that would have only confused the group.

"Romeo, huh? Not familiar with them," Leo mumbled.

The others turned to look at him with perplexed expressions. Why would he know any of them? Details on Enforcers were confidential. Only their code names were available to the public. Even details such as age, race, and gender were off the record. Of course, there was an underground organization dedicated to finding who they were but not much progress was made. It was almost as difficult as finding out who was involved in the Night of A Thousand Blades.

Leo realized the focus was on him, so he continued. "What happened after that?"

"He started to give a holier-than-thou speech. You know, the usual stuff. Probably would have started talking about the devil if a Primal didn't show up," Cassie said. She rubbed her arms as if to calm herself. The memories were still haunting. She already had a phobia of Primals and Fallen due to her history, and this incident made things much worse. The flow of events got so muddled when the monster appeared that Cassie struggled to differentiate between reality and fiction. A genuine nightmare took place for her. One that she couldn't wake from. One that was horrifyingly real.

"Odd. I saw the mess on my way back, but I never ran into a Primal. Did it run off after getting its fill?" Lyra asked. It was unsettling how calm she was about the explanation. Of course, she had an excellent reason for maintaining her composure during the reveal. She and the others had already assumed a Primal was involved. Only a mindless beast could leave such a scene. More than enough time had passed for the information to settle, so Lyra could speak about it matter-of-factly. Cassie was alone in her horror because she witnessed the crime firsthand. Then, there was the last important topic.

"Well… Alright, I know this sounds ridiculous… But I might have been saved by Tartarus at the last second," Cassie said. She was unsure if the others would believe her. What she was proposing was beyond ludicrous. A living legend came out of hiding after twenty years just to help a random girl? The very thought was baffling. Tartarus and the other commanders should have been enjoying lavish retirements by this point. Acting as vigilantes after etching their names in history seemed too hard to believe, yet no one questioned her.

"It is ridiculous. Commander of the Assault Battalion, Tartarus. A man who has no business wearing that mask anymore," Emma said. Her words were stern, though they followed the same monotone pattern they always did.

It wasn't hard to see why she disapproved of the commander's actions. All participants of the Night of A Thousand Blades were instructed to destroy the equipment they used that night. It was meant to both destroy evidence and prevent individuals from reusing such recognizable attire. Tartarus's appearance signaled to others that he went against such a basic order and risked encouraging them to do the same.

"Miss Emma, maybe it's best if we don't bad-mouth a commander. I mean, he got his position for a reason, right?" Sadie said, trying to ease the tension.

Naturally, people held different opinions over such a night. The event may have been for Evolved freedom, but many believed it could have been achieved with less bloodshed. None of the young adults present knew where Emma stood on the issue nor if she was one of the many masked participants. They also didn't dare to ask her.

"Irrelevant. Words will not wound him," Emma retorted. She didn't have the patience to argue with someone over a person who wasn't even in the room. Time could have been better spent elsewhere. More details were needed for a plan to be developed. Cassie's encounter with Enforcer Romeo meant that some Enforcers were prematurely enacting the Anti-Armament Law and murdering civilians. The event also showcased their usefulness against Primals. Emma may not have agreed with Tartarus's actions, but she admitted that only Evolved could handle a problem like this. She also understood that sending the children to fight was ruthlessly heartless, which is why she was surprised when one of them volunteered to do so.

"So, what should we do? I vote we chase down Tartarus. I... need to ask him a few things..." Cassie said. She wanted to veil the fact that the masked man used her real name. That small detail was the most unbelievable of all. She'd no doubt be ridiculed by the others, so Cassie opted to stay silent on the matter. The absence of this concerning fact led everyone to be lost on the sudden subject change. They couldn't believe their ears.

"What?! What could possibly be so important that you'd want to go back out there?! Here's what we should do. We should stay inside and let professionals deal with it," Leo said. He was bewildered. Why would Cassie even consider proposing such an idea? She was essentially asking everyone to go out on a suicide mission. Primals were not to be taken lightly, and Cassie had an overwhelming fear of them. She should have been scared for her life and begging to stay inside at all costs.

"Leo, calm down. Cassie, sweetie, I think you should reconsider. What do you even have to ask him anyway? It's not like he's related to us or anything. There's no way mom and dad could have known him," Lyra said. She earnestly tried to calm her two siblings. Her hand naturally reached to the feather pendant that hung from her neck. It still stung to bring up her parents, especially this close to the anniversary. She would have preferred not to, but Cassie wouldn't be deterred using anything less.

"Interesting," Emma mumbled underneath her breath. It had been many years since she'd seen the siblings squabble. The argument itself was valid. The problem was that all four siblings were stubborn in their own way. None of them would give up easily. There was also a sort of alliance between the twins that resulted in more uneven disputes. It was frustrating for both younger siblings who sometimes wanted to oppose their self-appointed proxy parents, leading to the formation of an alliance between them.

"Guys, I'm sure Cassie has a really good reason. We shouldn't shut her down without-" Orion tried to say but was interrupted.

"This isn't up for discussion, Junior!" Leo said, snapping at his brother.

"My name is Orion!" Orion shouted back. He never liked causing a commotion, but he also hated his nickname. It was a line that Leo knew not to cross, yet did so anyway. To be fair, the moment was too heated, and Orion's name change was relatively new. Leo wouldn't have said what he did in any other scenario. He knew how much the name meant to Orion. His irritation was the only reason why he stepped out of line. Thankfully, there was still an adult in the room.

"Enough," Emma said. She stood from her seat and jetted out her hands. Her back arched as her clothes tightened. Four large ichor constructs broke through her blouse not a moment later. Emma never wasted time showing off her Armament. She immediately had her four new limbs reach across the table and swept the bickering siblings off their feet. They tried to resist the expanding sticky ichor, but it was pointless. There was no escaping the spider's web. Soon, their mouths were sealed shut. Emma straightened her back and resumed her professional posture. "You are children. I will find Tartarus. Alone."

No one dared to argue with Emma, not that they could. Four of them were unable to speak, and the remaining two were smart enough to stay quiet. Even if they could protest, it was hard to find a better plan. Emma offered a solution that satisfied both parties and would guarantee results. She may not have been the best hunter in the world, but few could outmatch her in terms of stealth and traps. Her webs were a quick form of restraint that was difficult to break through, and her extra limbs added mobility. Altogether, Emma's plan was ironclad, but it still left Cassie feeling deflated. She wanted to find the answers for herself.

"Apologize to one another," Emma said. Her unnatural limbs slowly placed their victims back in their seats. The threads that bound them unraveled and slithered back to Emma. Once her Armament was retracted, her clothing began stitching itself together as if it were self-healing. The four siblings groaned their apologies, and Emma was left with a sense of nostalgia. Many years had passed since she had to pull a stunt like this to discipline her nieces and nephews.

That same nostalgia was more akin to irritation for the four that were forced to apologize. Each person still had their own opinion on what they believed the best option was, but they would never go against their aunt. At least, not in front of her.

⁂

Sadie and Audrey left the house not long after the dust had settled. Emma remained to force her charges to cooperate. She spent half of the day stitching together ruined clothes that the children had neglected. Both her mastery of her Armament and her rapid ichor regeneration led her to be an amazing seamstress that could produce a variety of self-repairing items. Of course, her pieces were far from cheap. The material was Emma's literal lifeblood and utilizing it as threads to make clothes was extremely taxing on her body. Her competition was also fairly weak, so she had free reign over the local market. The resounding success eventually led to the construction of a store in the Yellow Zone that was popular amongst both Evolved and humans.

The other half of Emma's day was spent critiquing her nieces and nephews. Some left their room a mess. Others hadn't properly cleaned the garage to make room for the cars to fit. The lawn needed to be mowed. The fans had to be dusted. Groceries were to be bought so the four siblings didn't have to eat the same meals over and over again. Then, there was the constant usage of Emma's ichor threads when she monitored the others. She frequently startled them with her silent movements and carelessly left discarded strands of ichor on the floor, which then needed to be swept. It didn't take long for the four siblings to forget their dispute and ally against a common irritant. They almost couldn't contain their excitement once the sun set and Emma left to hunt Tartarus.

Leo and Lyra waited for several minutes before nodding to each other. They quickly left Orion and Cassie in the living room to retreat to their rooms. The sounds of drawers opening and slamming shut echoed through the silent house for several minutes. The noises soon stopped, and the twins reemerged from their respective rooms. They had donned dark clothing and guards that offered a small amount of protection. Gloves and boots capped their extremities, and masks from last year's Halloween party were reused to hide their identities. The twins double-checked their equipment before heading toward the backdoor.

"Aunt Emma's going to be pissed," Orion said. He shook his head to the others and gave them a concerned expression that said, *are you serious?* What the twins were planning was painfully obvious. The fake smiles they wore finally came off as they prepared to stand their ground. Neither one of them would be deterred so easily. Fighting a Primal would have been extremely difficult for them, but there was no doubt that the twins could best their younger siblings.

"So, I still don't get my way, and you two just run around doing whatever you want? Tell me how that's fair," Cassie said with an irritated voice. She could barely hold back the barrage of insults that flooded her mind. She was livid. Quick feet took her off the couch. Leo and Lyra reacted similarly. Both made a mad dash to the door. They couldn't risk being trapped in the house. It was much easier to escape Cassie if they entered the city and separated. This way, they could satisfy Cassie's need to question Tartarus without putting her in danger. The twins naively believed they could help their aunt with the search despite being explicitly told to stay indoors.

"Cassie, hold on!" Orion said. He rushed toward his sister with outstretched arms. He detested picking sides, especially against his younger sister, but this was important. A simple grab of the sleeve was all Orion needed to stop Cassie. Leo and Lyra took advantage of the distraction and slipped out of the house unimpeded. Now, every second exponentially added to the difficulty Cassie would have in relocating them. She turned to her brother with a menacing glare. She tightly clenched her shaking fists. Fearing the justified repercussions, Orion immediately explained himself. "Aunt Emma set a trap!"

He desperately held up his hands and cowered away from the fist that stopped mid-swing. He knew all about Emma's plan. During the day's onslaught of chores, Orion witnessed her stringing together delicate threads of ichor. They were much too small to notice in the dark of night, and they broke easily to stick to whoever tore through them. Every possible exit was rigged with these invisible wires. Emma likely planned to check them once she returned from her expedition. If she found one was broken, she would search the siblings and quickly identify the culprit.

Cassie contemplated what she was told. The wires immediately snapped when an exit was opened. Those same ichor wires latched onto who broke through them. Using basic logic, Cassie quickly figured out the system's loophole. She could escape through the same exit as Leo and Lyra. Those two already triggered the trap and got themselves tagged. As long as Cassie left and returned through the backdoor as well, Emma wouldn't know she ever left. All evidence would only point to the twins. The plan was almost foolproof. A bone-chilling grin spread across her face. She could get all that she wanted. She would be able to hunt Tartarus, and her arrogant older siblings would be alone when they faced Emma's wrath.

"So, all we have to do is use the backdoor. This is perfect! We can go after them! Come on, let's go!" Cassie said. She ran to her room and shuffled through her belongings. She didn't have time to completely change her wardrobe, nor would her wings allow an oversized outfit. Her options were limited, so she stuck to the basics. She grabbed her personal AE pocket knife just in case she would be forced to fight.

Running shoes were hastily tightened, and her shirt was changed for one that better accommodated her Armament.

"Nononononono. We can't go out there," Orion said almost immediately. He was also angry at the twins, but he agreed with them on the fact that Cassie had no business going outside. She still had a paralyzing fear of Primals, and one continued to roam the city's darkest corners. Enforcer Romeo reported that he shot down an Evolved with wings and then went missing soon after, so his partners were likely looking for her to enact revenge. Lastly, Cassie was still recovering. She wasn't completely healed yet. Orion could go on and on about why his little sister was insane but kept the explanation short.

"Then I'll go alone," Cassie said with a hint of sorrow. The one person she expected to support her was now trying to hold her back. Orion stood at the doorway to block his sister's only escape. He didn't like confrontation, but he also knew he couldn't let her leave. Cassie knelt down and began digging through her backpack. Her eyes locked with her brother's as she mumbled, "Get out of the way."

"No, we can just-" Orion tried to say, but his sentence was cut off. He was too kind. He let his guard down because he thought he could reason with his sister.

Unfortunately, her mind was too focused to listen to any type of reasoning. Cassie instinctively threw her heavy backpack when she heard the denial. The attack alone wasn't very impressive. Orion caught the bag before it struck his face and took a step back to balance himself. He peered over the makeshift weapon only to see Cassie rushing him. His arms immediately brought the bag down to block the knee strike aimed at his stomach. The rapid response was praise-worthy, but it also left his upper body unguarded. Cassie took advantage of this mistake and struck her brother with a jab to the temple.

She spun on her heels and desperately sprinted toward the kitchen, tripping over her own feet. She wasn't used to indoor combat, nor did she believe she could win against any of her siblings in a direct confrontation. Her only hope was to escape Orion's range so he couldn't shoot her out of the sky. Unfortunately, that was easier said than done. Her baffled brother was far from helpless, and he would do anything to keep his sister inside.

One of his now-infamous rope shots raced through the hall and caught Cassie's thigh. He was still reeling from the punch, but his aim was impeccable nonetheless. The ichor rope tightened and swept its victim off her feet. Cassie recoiled from the pain. She could feel the barbed projectile whenever she moved. It felt as if a chunk of her leg would be torn off if she was careless. She grabbed the rope to fight against it without causing more damage. The two siblings then began their small game of tug of war, but one was prepared to cut the game short.

Not wanting to waste any more time, Cassie ruffled through her pockets to retrieve her AE knife. The blade flicked out of its handle and glimmered like a magnificent amethyst gemstone. Being from an expensive material, few people had their own personal AE equipment. That was why Enforcers and high-ranking officials were the only people to have a large supply. Even small items like the one Cassie held were expensive. Still, it was a gift from her late father. One that he allegedly stole back in his younger days. He eventually gave it to Cassie for her to defend herself, but he probably never would have guessed it'd be used against one of her siblings.

Cassie swiped through the ichor rope with ease. The connection between the two siblings was severed, and they both fell back from the sudden lack of pulling. Cassie refused to wait for the next shot. She clenched her teeth and yanked the arrow out of her leg. Pain lingered where the object was once embedded in her, but it was quickly subsiding. Compared to the AE pellets she was shot with, this was nothing. Her relatively weak regeneration would be enough to heal her without relying on Nectar.

Meanwhile, Orion's attack potential dropped. His average damage per second was cut in half while he was forced to regenerate another rope shot. Most of the ichor used in the first shot was now wasted and needed to be reconfigured. A new tethered arrow would need to be prepared, which cost both time and energy. Of course, nothing was ever slow for an Evolved. Generating his next projectile would take a minute at most, but that was more than enough time for Cassie to fly out of his range. Orion knew this and readied to utilize his other arm's arrow as effectively as possible. He'd need to delay his sister as much as possible to regain his innate advantage.

Move! Cassie thought to herself as she tried to press forward. She shoved both her knife and the barbed arrow into her pocket. All she had to do now was escape the house. Ichor was finite, so Orion's tethered arrows couldn't sail endlessly into the night sky. He also wouldn't fire his regular shots because any that missed would become a liability. Knowing those two things, Cassie rushed for the backdoor. Her unbalanced legs forced her to bounce off of the walls as she stumbled to the exit. She rammed open the door without any regret and immediately summoned her wings.

An overwhelming sensation of freedom filled her as she soared through the air. The rush of exhilaration made her want to try to touch the moon, but a piercing pain snapped her back into reality. Orion's desperate attempt to stop his sister took the form of yet another roped arrow. His other arm still needed time to prepare its next shot, so it held onto the nearby door frame and acted as an anchor. This was his only opportunity to restrain Cassie. He couldn't take any chances. He immediately put all of his efforts into reeling his sister back to earth.

Cassie couldn't understand why her brother was so hellbent on stopping her. He wasn't anywhere near this desperate to prevent Leo and Lyra from leaving. He certainly didn't try to keep Emma from hunting Tartarus and the Primal. It simply wasn't in his nature. Orion refrained from opposing people and bristled at the idea of conflict with his family members. He'd much rather take the loss than create animosity between him and the others. This was especially true with Cassie. The two were close because of their perceived lower position within the family. So, why was Orion frantically trying to keep Cassie from leaving that night? It was yet another question that she'd soon find the answer to.

Regardless of what her brother was thinking, Cassie needed to leave. She twisted her body to wrap the ichor rope around her anchored leg. The writhing pain began to expand as the arrowhead shifted, but it lessened when most of the thread was tangled around her lower half. Orion continued to pull but to no avail. The arrow was no longer jostling about thanks to Cassie's quick thinking. She could finally fight against her brother on even ground. The two went back and forth for what felt like an eternity. Orion could practically feel his ichor being yanked out of his body, and Cassie's wings grew tired with each pull. Even so, neither side was willing to concede.

The struggle was intense but direct. It became more of a battle of strength and momentum than anything else. At least, that was what Orion thought. He became too focused on the game of tug of war once again. He may have readied himself for the inevitable event when the rope snapped, but he never expected Cassie to suddenly shift her weight and fly straight up. His iron grip faltered as it became increasingly difficult to hold on to the doorframe. Before he knew it, Orion was swept off his feet. The two siblings soared through the air, and the house below became worryingly small. Regret immediately set in the flightless brother as he stared at the ground.

Cassie refused to allow her brother to think of an escape. She accelerated further to increase her altitude until the two reached the perfect height. Her graceful wings fully expanded to halt her momentum, but Orion continued his course. Cassie gritted her teeth and pulled out the object embedded in her. It may not have been the worst pain she'd felt recently but she certainly preferred if this was the last. She maneuvered herself in mid-air to bypass Orion as he flew by. A sudden thrust from her wings put her in the perfect position. It didn't take long for him to realize what was happening. He tried to resist, but it was too late. Cassie was a master of aerial combat. She circled him several times with the tethered arrow in hand. Orion watched helplessly as his weapon was used against him. His arms and legs became tangled in the ichor, forming a mess that couldn't be unraveled.

Once Orion was completely restrained, Cassie stabbed the arrow she held into his shoulder as a form of payback for earlier. She was satisfied with her smaller amount of vengeance but wanted a tad bit more. Her grip loosened as she gave her brother a courteous smile. Gravity pulled him back down at an alarming speed. The wind that rushed past him was deafening. Orion tried his best to escape. He desperately wanted to minimize the damage that would be done on impact. His eyes darted toward his sister. She was also free-falling, but her descent could always be safely stopped with her wings. The same wasn't true for Orion, who continued to flail and worm around in the air. The ground expanded as he came closer to his crash landing with each second. When all of his struggles proved futile, he shut his eyes and braced for the worst.

Then, he came to a sudden stop.

The ichor rope around him tightened, especially around his midsection. Cassie was kind enough to prevent her brother from embedding a permanent silhouette into the ground. She snickered at his fearful face and dropped him from a much safer height. Orion was still scared of falling, but this descent was much easier to handle. He landed on the ground with an audible thump before bouncing. His bindings still held him, so Orion began rolling around as he continued his struggle for freedom. That same fight against his shackles only made the situation worse for him. Naturally, he was livid. His younger sister had practically made a mockery of him, and she floated above as if to tease him. In reality, Cassie was watching to make sure he wouldn't escape. She quickly realized she was safe and decided to finally begin her mission.

The night was colder than Cassie initially expected. She was under-dressed, and the wind that rushed by as she flew didn't help. That was simply the trade-off for such a unique Armament. Not many people could brag about having wings, but those same people found solace in their ability to wear warm clothing. Of course, she did have some custom-made clothes that took her wings into account.

The only problem was that she left without them. The panicked rush out the door and subsequent fight left her with little time to prepare. Cassie debated on returning home but quickly dismissed that idea. It would be too embarrassing to return and waltz past her ensnared brother just for a jacket. Her cool renegade facade would be ruined. So, she decided to continue with her current objective.

The mission was straightforward: find Tartarus and ask him a series of questions. Was he the real Tartarus? How was he affiliated with her? Why was he active after being dormant for so many years? They were the most basic of questions that she could think of, a good starting point. The answers would only satisfy her momentarily and generate plenty of new queries. If she could, she would ask plenty more. Of course, that all hinged on her ability to track and extract information from the old commander.

Cassie's main concern stemmed from Leo and Lyra's current position. Those two should have been patrolling the area. Much to the annoyance of their little sister, they were looking for the commander as well. The chance of crossing paths with one another was high, and Cassie had no way of detecting or monitoring them. She decided to avoid this issue by staying well above the towering buildings. It was best to stay out of their sight. Plus, if they did spot her, they would never be able to reach her.

Finding one person in the middle of the night was difficult. Tartarus's cryptic nature and the time of day both hindered the search. Not even Cassie's bird's-eye view offered much help. The process was troublesome because he could be anyone underneath the mask. No one knew who the commander was. That fact was daunting, but it also brought a bit of solace to Cassie. It meant that her older siblings were probably also facing a seemingly impossible task. The circular flight pattern wasn't producing results fast enough, so Cassie decided to investigate where the previous night's encounter took place.

She initially wanted to avoid the area because either of her siblings or Emma might have been there. She was extremely cautious when she landed on a nearby rooftop. Her head swiveled as she searched for anyone that might resemble a family member. Fortunately, there was no one. Cassie was free to gaze down into the alley where she once thought she'd die.

The deceased, and mostly eaten, Enforcer had been removed. A chalk outline etched his silhouette into the ground, including the parts of him that were missing or tossed aside. Most paths to the area had been blocked to prevent anyone from tampering with the crime scene. Guards were stationed at the taped-off entrances to ward off curious eyes, but they failed to notice the two individuals that were already within the area. Cassie stood still on the roof, with a lone person standing on the ground below.

This strange woman was dressed in a crimson suit. Her outfit was well-tailored and conformed to her body. The yellow and red striped tie that hung from her neck bounced around as she searched the alley. Her outer extremities were covered with gloves and boots to completely veil any potential identifiable features. In any other scenario, Cassie would immediately assume this woman was a high-profile individual. The only thing that kept her from solidifying that belief was the odd helmet that prominently stood out. The woman wore a metal helmet that closely followed the contours of her face. No details were etched into the material to give it personality, so its sole unique feature was its color. The chin of the mask was an eye-catching amber that slowly morphed into a deep maroon, closely resembling a sunrise.

Another one, Cassie thought. She squinted at the woman below. Given her attire, it was clear that she was associated with Tartarus in some way. Was she another participant in the Night of A Thousand Blades? It was certainly possible. Too many people joined in on the event to track all of them. Plenty of those unknown people could have kept their masks or remade them once they saw Tartarus. The very thought was troubling. Not only were there more mysterious individuals to worry about, but they might prevent Cassie from hunting the commander.

She decided to continue analyzing the situation by watching the stranger below. The masked woman poked around the crime scene without a single worry about being seen. The lack of local law enforcement certainly helped. The few officers that remained in the area were exhausted and overworked. Their minds were also frantic with the thought of a Primal running amok, so Cassie wasn't surprised to see them stay away from one of the city's darkest corners.

It wasn't immediately clear what the masked woman was doing. She was simply meandering around. If she had a tracking Armament, she might have been looking for something to help her search for the Primal. It would have been a great plan if the police and Enforcers hadn't picked the scene clean. It was also viable that she was acting as bait for when the Primal inevitably returned for more food. Whatever she was doing likely hinged on her Armament, which was impossible to predict. Viewing her Emblem might have given a hint to Cassie, but her body was veiled by her high-class outfit.

Cassie began to regret that she wasn't a better student in school. She could have been much more diligent. If she was, she would have known more details about the Night of A Thousand Blades than was generally known. At the time, she didn't think it was necessary to study a recent major event that everyone knew about. It was naive to assume she knew everything. She might have known the woman or at least her associated battalion had she paid more attention in class.

Those thoughts quickly came to a halt once the veiled figure moved. The masked woman had finished whatever job she was sent to do and casually stepped away from the crime scene. Quiet steps took her through the alley, going deeper into the dense concrete jungle that was the Red Zone's center. The woman moved with complete confidence as if she knew every inch of the city. Meanwhile, Cassie followed her target from the roofs above. Her optimal position allowed her to pursue the woman with ease. That is, until something upset her.

The once peaceful walk unexpectedly turned into a full sprint, and the chase commenced. Cassie's quiet steps shifted to stumbling wing-assisted leaps as she tried to keep pace. The pursuit grew more difficult as the buildings began varying in size. The space between each structure was also inconsistent, displaying how poorly the zone's infrastructure was planned. Exhaustion quickly sat in. Cassie was weighed down by her sore wings and the numerous low-altitude feats she had to perform. She would have loved to sail into the sky, but that wasn't an option at the moment. She didn't know if the woman began running because she saw the winged girl or if she'd heard something from the streets below. It would have been naive to reveal herself prematurely. For now, Cassie decided to act under the assumption that she was still hidden.

The masked woman continued her calculated path. She sprinted down alleys, expertly weaved through obstacles, and made several nonsensical turns. The tedious run proved to be difficult for Cassie, but it ended after a few minutes. The woman finally arrived at her destination. It was a small apartment complex that drowned in a sea of significantly taller buildings. Unlike Fee's Oasis, this structure didn't have the luxury of a street-side view or open area for people to congregate. Only a few alleyways big enough for a car to fit through existed, but most people would avoid venturing to such a remote place. Given its surroundings, the complex was impossible to find and largely forgotten about. One would either have to know about it beforehand or have a bird's-eye view like Cassie did to locate it.

It was the perfect place for people to meet in secret.

The masked woman glanced around to see if anyone was nearby. Of course, this area was vacant. Someone would have to be incredibly lost to discover such a place, yet she checked. Cassie hid as best she could, worried about how her plan would crumble if she were spotted. Fortunately, the woman seemed to be more worried about a potential presence on the ground. She stepped closer to the building as she searched her coat. A shining set of keys reflected the moon's light as they twirled around her fingers. No longer concerned about others, she casually loosened her tie before opening the building's front doors. A faint light radiated from the unseen room, and a shadow danced when she entered the complex.

Cassie was left dumbstruck. She only intended to meet Tartarus. She never planned on following one of his companions let alone finding their hideout. The scope of this group was quickly becoming more obvious and worrying. Cassie finally felt like she overstepped her boundaries. This was in a realm far from the normal life she lived. Whoever these people were, they were dangerous and unpredictable. They were likely planning something grand if they were wearing their old outfits from over twenty years ago. An endless amount of questions popped into Cassie's mind about the group and its mission. She clearly got more than she bargained for when she originally left her home. Her wings stretched out to prepare for departure. The best plan was to return at a later date with more information and support from the others.

The wind blew as Cassie rose from the ground. Normally, it took little effort for her to soar above the highest buildings. Her altitude always rose substantially with a single thrust, but this movement was impossible. Something had gripped the back of her shirt and yanked her back, snapping her head forward. Cassie twisted to prevent her collar from choking her. Her angered wings flapped relentlessly to fight against the binds that held the body. Fearful eyes locked onto what had gripped her. She was worried about the Primal returning, but it proved to be something even more concerning.

Two new masked individuals presented themselves. They somehow managed to quietly appear where Cassie once stood. Much like the two before them, both newcomers were equipped with tailored formal attire that somewhat matched their odd headwear. Whether they were also participants in the infamous night didn't matter anymore. This group was obviously organized, and it was reasonable to assume they would do anything to maintain their hidden agenda.

The person holding Cassie was a woman with an interesting Armament. Her hand extended from her wrist with a trail of ichor connecting the two, reaching far enough to hold her prey with ease. Small bones could be spotted along the stretched arm that closely mirrored those of a snake. Aside from the woman's white button-up shirt, each piece of her outfit utilized a print with a variety of shapes and colors. The design was reminiscent of geometric art, but it also followed a more modern palette that one would see at a rave. Her mask was equally fascinating, consisting of only a handful of edges. This item heavily resembled a poorly rendered 3D fox head. Each plate of the low poly mask was colored similarly to her suit and utilized its uniform shadows to add an extra layer of depth.

Compared to the woman, the veiled man could be considered normal. He wore an extremely formal tuxedo which heavily clashed against his partner's vivid colors. One wouldn't think twice if they saw him at a formal event. His apparel was free from any blemishes and made him look sleek. This professional look was complemented by a tie with the words "Memento Mori" stitched into it with fine calligraphy. Matching the theme of this tie was the mask he wore. It was made of white agate which was expertly crafted into the shape of a skull. Ornate details were painted in black and followed a typical Día de Los Muertos style. This blend of death and beauty was captivating to see, but the man was not in the mood to pose elegantly. He stood with crossed arms as his companion reeled in her catch. The man almost looked disappointed, but it was impossible to tell given the circumstances.

Cassie thrashed against the arm that anchored her and flapped her wings violently. Her mind raced for ideas of escape. She wanted to detach the hand that clung to her, but she didn't want to reveal what she was capable of yet. She couldn't let them know she had an AE knife. That was because Evolved-on-Evolved combat typically revolved around information.

Knowing another person's Armament and weapons meant that strategies could be formed to circumnavigate them. The group probably knew about Cassie through Tartarus, so someone with the ability to hold her was dispatched. The same could likely be said about the masked man, who had yet to move. Did he also have a restraining technique, or was he only there to chase her if she escaped? Regardless, the cards had been dealt. Cassie might have exposed her wings prematurely, but she refused to expose her hidden blade. She desperately threw together a plan. It was far from perfect but was also her only chance.

Everything would be settled in one critical move.

The skull-masked man stepped forward as Cassie collected herself. He believed she was struggling in vain, but she was far from helpless. She mentally prepared herself as the arm finished reeling her onto the roof. Cassie knew she needed to resist. Her flailing was pathetic, to the point where the man felt sorry for her. It was a well-played facade that he fell for immediately.

Cassie's fight against the woman was easier now that she was on the ground, but it wasn't even a fair competition. She was losing ground fast. She pumped her legs to combat the pulling force and inch away from the man that approached her. The struggle was intense for her, but boring for the other two. To them, it was like watching a child throw a tantrum. She'd soon run out of energy and accept defeat. At least, that was what they assumed. They never expected Cassie to subtly reach into her pocket. This would be her biggest gamble.

She split the two items she held to grasp one in each hand. Her grip tightened as she waited for the precise moment to strike. Her heart thumped louder than ever before as she timed her next attack. *One.* The man came closer. *Two.* The woman pulled even harder. *Three!* Cassie arched her wings back, stretching them as far as she could. She threw her wings forward to send a gust of wind. At the same time, she threw an object that she was more than willing to lose.

Orion's stolen arrowhead left her hand and flew toward the masked duo. Startled, the skull-masked man leapt in front of his companion to block the attack. Even professionally trained combatants would be thrown off by a sudden change. One projectile was enough to put Cassie's opponent on the defensive as they wondered if there was more to her Armament. They didn't have time to register that it was simply something she threw recklessly.

She used the distraction as an opportunity to throw herself off the building. The ichor arm that held her stretched as it slowed her descent, stopping her from hitting the ground. Cassie refused to wait for the woman to let go of her voluntarily. She flicked out her AE knife and sliced at her enemy. A blood-curdling cry rang out as the excruciating pain reached the woman. Evolved may have had rapid regeneration and high defenses, but that didn't negate the pain they felt. The woman's arm was practically torn to shreds. It had no choice but to release its grip.

Cassie wasted no time rising to her feet. She stumbled down the alleyway. No doubt a rage-fueled chase would soon occur. Cassie's reputation with the group would plummet to its lowest, but she didn't care. She just needed to enter a populated area. The Red Zone was nothing if not full of Evolved. People were bound to help a distressed girl in a situation like this. The group that chased her was trying to remain hidden, so they wouldn't dare follow her onto the main streets and risk fighting bystanders. Frantic legs carried Cassie as fast as they could. She believed she could get away. The time she bought should have been enough. Her ragged breath was proof that she was escaping them.

She was wrong.

"Sorry, kid," a calm voice said. No, it was two voices that spoke in unison. A pair of similarly dressed men stepped out of the shadows, cutting off Cassie's escape. She tried to see who they were, but a set of hands covered her eyes. The two men worked together and pushed their palms into her face with an absurd amount of force. They firmly guided the panicking girl to the ground, crushing her into the concrete with an audible thud.

Cassie's vision was hazy after the impact. She tried to move, but her body was unresponsive. It took every ounce of focus to get a glimpse of the men that had captured her. Just as everything became clear, the dark side of a heel filled her view.

Chapter 4: Subgiant

A soft light crept through a series of dense curtains and blinds, dimly lighting a small room that was neatly decorated yet barren. Dressers and bookshelves lined the walls, but they were empty. A large black and white patterned rug covered most of the wooden floor. Two comfortable slippers rested at the foot of the bed that sat in the room's corner. It would have been a nice place to live if it weren't currently caging someone.

The rays of early morning sunshine warmed both the bed and the young woman resting in it. Cassie tossed and turned for a bit, grumbling harsh words at whatever woke her up. If she could turn off the sun, she would. She preferred to sleep. This was one of the few times she could properly rest. No nightmares haunted her. All she dreamt of was darkness, and she'd rather have stayed there than face reality. Unfortunately, that was no longer an option.

Cassie's eyes fluttered open, but residual fatigue tried to lull her back to sleep. The wings that were never fully retracted felt sore from a night of heavy slumber and awkward positions. Pain still lingered from where she met concrete and the negative end of a stomp. The previous night's events stuck in her mind. Her eyes widened as she frantically looked around. She needed to leave this place immediately. She had no idea what the masked group had planned for her, but she knew her survival rate increased exponentially once she was out of the building.

Her worried eyes darted around. She had never seen this room before. It was cozy yet empty, as if unprepared for a guest to arrive so soon. Given the event leading up to this situation, Cassie safely assumed that she was in the building she saw the previous night. The masked people must have brought her into the apartment complex and locked her in a spare room after knocking her unconscious. They likely had a solid reason for this, but Cassie wasn't interested in learning it. A few stretches were all she needed to drum up motivation and clear any remaining exhaustion. With the most minimal of preparations in place, she locked her eyes on the door across the room.

Quiet feet desperately tried to avoid causing the wooden floor to creak. Cassie's wings retracted as she checked her pockets. Of course, everything was gone. Her AE knife was stolen as was her phone, so she had no way to defend herself nor contact the outside world. Priority went to fleeing the facility, but Cassie certainly wouldn't complain if she stumbled upon her belongings. The irritation she felt over losing her items slowly faded when she realized how grave the situation was. She could have easily been tied up and thrown in some random basement, if not killed.

The walk toward the door seemed to go on forever due to the overwhelming sense of dread that filled Cassie. Her breathing steadily slowed as she collected herself. She reflected on her dilemma. At the moment, there was no definitive number of masked people within the building. She had encountered six members of the group so far, but more of them could be lingering in the shadows. Most details of the apartment complex were hidden as well. Cassie decided to believe her situation was grim. She assumed she was on the highest floor possible and that at least half of the masked team was on the premises at any given time.

She took one final deep breath to calm herself. Blind fear and speculation would only defeat her before her real enemies could. She had to remind herself that she was an Evolved, too. True, her ability was better suited for open areas, but that meant that Cassie only needed to exit the building. No one she had met so far was leagues above her. Every fight she had lost recently was due to the element of surprise. Now, she had a plan. She roughly knew what she was up against and figured out how to handle them. It was finally her time to shine.

Cassie pressed her ear against the room's only door. She held her breath to listen closely. Anything, even the slightest hint of movement, would send her into a defensive position. Moments passed as she waited for a sound, but there was nothing. The next room was eerily silent. Had she really been left alone? Cassie shook her head. It was far too early to think that. Someone on the other side could be using a stealth-like Armament. She clenched her fist to remind herself to stay vigilant. A steady hand cautiously opened the door. Every effort was put into keeping the door relatively silent. She didn't want to risk a rogue squeak alerting her watchers. Once it was open enough, Cassie slipped through the door and closed it behind her.

She checked her surroundings to confirm that she was, in fact, alone. A sigh of relief escaped her. She secretly hoped all transitions would be like this. Her much calmer eyes scanned the room. To her immediate right was a window with curtains and blinds opened wide. Light burst through the glass to illuminate the hall. Cassie glanced outside to notice she was on the second floor. She turned her head and noted the empty chair and water bottle that sat at the end of the hallway. Next to those two out-of-place items was an open door leading to an indoor stairwell. Aside from the room Cassie just left, three other rooms remained closed.

After looking at all her options, it seemed like the window would lead to the fastest escape. That was all she needed. Broken shards of glass and potential bad luck weren't enough to deter her from taking the easiest route. Of course, it would have been better to try the window in the prior room, but her tunnel vision got the best of her. Cassie pressed her hand against the glass before applying pressure. She pushed with all of her might, but nothing happened. Odd. Even the weakest Evolved could break glass with an iota of strength. So, why was this so hard? She grew more frustrated with each failed attempt to quietly break the glass. A clenched fist formed and crashed into the window. Cassie expected to break through, but the opposite happened. Pain coursed through her hand as it recoiled from the impact.

Gah! I don't know if it's reinforced or tempered glass, but damn that hurts! Cassie thought as she soothed the throbbing sensation in her knuckles. It seemed like no expense was spared when it came to this building's construction. That should have been obvious. Why would a battalion commander operate in a run-down facility? This fortress was probably amazing, but Cassie could only see it as an intimidating prison. She turned in a huff and moved on to the next method of escape.

Quiet steps carried her down the hallway. She held her breath as she crept by each door. The nervousness that filled her quickly overshadowed any other thought she had. Someone could pop out at any moment. There was no way to confirm if those rooms were occupied without peeking in, but Cassie was nowhere near brave enough to do that. All she wanted was to escape without seeing anyone. She tried to remain vigilant as she reached the empty chair next to the stairwell. She steeled herself and prepared for anything. A quick hop took her out of the hallway.

But the wooden floor behind her creaked and forced her to stop.

Cassie twisted so fast that she almost wrenched her back. Scared eyes frantically looked for someone, but there was nobody in the hall. The four doors remained closed. The chair and water bottle hadn't moved. Everything was the same, yet it felt as if a new presence was in the room. She took a step back. Something didn't feel right. The shadows on the floor didn't match with their surroundings, and what stood out was dangerously close to her.

Before Cassie could react, an invisible force pressed against her chest. The push wasn't particularly strong, but its surprise sent Cassie reeling. She stumbled back and feverishly attempted to stay upright. Unfortunately, it was all in vain. The same invisible force pressed against her stomach and sent her tumbling down the stairs. Cassie crashed against the bottom step and slammed her face against the wall at the bottom. She heard the footsteps that followed her, but there was still no figure.

A quick battle stance was assumed. She knew she had to put up a fight. Just because her enemy was invisible didn't mean they were unhittable. Cassie tried to picture her opponent. She imagined this was a shadow boxing drill. The clicking footsteps came closer. Whoever this was, they no longer saw the need to stay quiet. Cassie smiled. That worked in her favor. The faint image of another person flickered in her imagination. They were right in front of her. Cassie's eyes narrowed as she blindly sent out an amateur right hook. To her surprise, her attack landed. To her misfortune, what she hit was incredibly hard. The soft sound of metal ringing could be heard, and her knuckles began to bleed.

Whoever took the pitiful punch decided to drop the act and disable their incredible Armament. A woman materialized out of thin air. Her entire body had been veiled in a specialized blend of ichor. The light it reflected acted as a rudimentary cloaking mechanism, but it wasn't perfect. Slight shimmers of her figure could be seen if one focused enough, and it didn't prevent shadows from forming. Those simple flaws could easily ruin the woman's ability to hide. Fortunately, her opponent panicked and didn't register every detail perfectly.

Following the formulaic trend, this woman was dressed in formal attire which was accompanied by odd headgear. Her suit heavily contrasted her Armament by being an overbearingly bright white. Steel boots and gauntlets covered the ends of her extremities, and a medieval knight helmet sat on her head. Its front plate came to a sharp point with a noticeable dent where Cassie struck it. The narrow opening for eyesight was covered in a dark material that only allowed vision from one side. Long flowing blonde hair sprouted from the bottom and elegantly bounced with each step. The woman would have been an enchanting sight if she didn't currently have such an intimidating aura.

Are you serious?! They can turn invisible, too?! Cassie thought. She started to panic. Countless Armaments existed among the Evolved population, and rarity often meant strength. People with unique abilities were idolized and often considered more powerful than others. Of course, wings capable of flight were a sight to behold. Cassie was also the object of envy within the mobile-type community. She was only frustrated because of her current situation. Those amazing assets of hers were worthless at the moment.

Cassie tried to recall all the people she knew with outstanding Armaments. Unfortunately, most of the people she knew were somewhat generic. Only a handful of individuals stood out against a sea of normality. The closest person to the woman before her was a certain nonchalant and brutally honest friend, but the two couldn't be the same. There was a noticeable lack of motivation, and she'd never join an odd group like this. It would cut into her invaluable free time. Before Cassie could fully explore that avenue of thought, she was kicked into the next room and snapped back into reality.

Unlike the second floor, the bottom floor consisted of a single large room with multiple pillars for support. Across the room was a second stairwell which likely led to a similar hall and set of rooms. Cassie's eyes were immediately drawn to the array of monitors on the far wall. An impressively huge screen sat at the center and detailed a map of the city. Several smaller screens circled their grander counterpart, providing supplementary data ranging from weather to mission details.

A beautifully handcrafted round table rested in the middle of the room. Nine hand-held devices sat in the front of each seat, displaying data that correlated to the screens. The center of the table was hollowed out to fit a modern device that displayed a hologram projection of the city's landscape. The image visualized the different zones by utilizing their respective colors, and bright dots marked points of interest. Seated at the head of the table was the man in charge of everything.

Tartarus read through his tablet, patiently waiting for his guest to arrive. His suit was as sharp as ever, and the gears on his mask continued to quietly tick like before. He firmly held his device while he scrolled through the meeting's notes. Today's topics were important and would shape the group's future. No point was too small to scrutinize.

Sitting to his immediate left was the red-helmeted woman. She was also quietly reading through her notes, but her focus was derailed by the sudden commotion. She nearly jumped out of her seat when Cassie burst into the room. Her companion, the invisible woman, showed no remorse for the interruption and silently waltzed after her prey. She gave a courteous nod before pulling her victim to the table and tossing her into the seat across from the leader. A cruel grip kept her in place, conflicting with the warm welcome Tartarus gave.

"It seems like you've finally woken up. Did you sleep well?" Tartarus asked with a voice full of concern for his captive's well-being. It was odd to hear that tone from the leader of the people that kidnapped her. He waved his hand to signal Cassie's release, and the invisible woman immediately let go. She took several steps back and then walked over to her appropriate seat, directly right of Tartarus. Cassie, meanwhile, sat in stark silence. She wasn't sure how to respond. Was it better to be friendly or demand a way out of this mess? No clear answer presented itself, so Cassie defaulted to the only thing she was verbally ready for.

"Are you the real Tartarus? What's with the new group? What will you do with me? Better yet, how do you know me? Are those two questions related to each other? Wait, are we related to each other? Also, did you get attacked by a creepy spider lady last night?" Cassie stammered. Her mind was blank. She spat out every pre-prepared question she had. Panic and stress had set in once again. Her thoughts somehow managed to race so fast that they practically spiraled out of control. Fortunately, the victim of all these questions handled them confidently.

"I am the real Tartarus, the current active leader of the Celestials. We are a group dedicated to dealing with the growing Primal threat. You simply happened to find our base of operations while everyone was returning from their patrols and got swept up in the moment. I'm sorry for their actions." Tartarus gave a slight bow at the end. He had conveniently skipped over Cassie's most important questions, but the answers provided drew her attention. The group's goals seemed rather lofty and altruistic. Primals and Fallen weren't simple problems that could be handled by amateurs. Even the government was slow to handle the issue.

"I am Hemera, Alpha Team Leader of the Celestials," the red-helmeted woman said. "You know, sweetheart, you really shouldn't follow strangers in the middle of the night. Didn't your family teach you better than that?" Her voice was modified thanks to a hidden device within her mask, but her motherly nature still came across.

The bit of teasing reminded Cassie of her own family. Simply thinking of them tugged at her heart. What were they thinking right now? They were probably worried beyond belief that she never returned home. They might have even thought that she was dead.

"I'm Nike, Bravo Team Leader of the Celestials. I'd rather boot you out of here, but the boss has a request for you. Don't worry. You're probably going to turn it down, anyways. Then, we'll send you home," the previously invisible woman said. She crossed her arms as if to emphasize her objection to Cassie's presence. Not even the distortion of her voice could hide her unwarranted irritation. Although, the two had no reason to be enemies, they had met mere minutes ago. This hostility, however, was somewhat calming to Cassie. She found solace in the fact that not everyone was vying for her affection.

The three masked individuals had finally managed to introduce themselves with varying degrees of success. It was a mediocre start, but plenty more could have been said. The scope of the group could be covered. Tartarus could explain why he was the only person who neglected to use a voice modifier. There was also a noticeable lack of evidence on how they planned to stop the Primal epidemic. The research for that alone had to be expensive and daunting, so they must have gotten a large amount of funding from somewhere. Cassie wished they said more, but a certain level of respect was needed first and foremost.

"It's an honor to meet you, sir. I'm sure I speak on behalf of all Evolved when I say thank you for all that you've done as the Assault Battalion Commander," Cassie said with an extremely formal voice.

A level of distrust continued to persist, but the introductions alleviated some of the animosity. That was the formidable power of a battalion commander's name. Any one of the five commanders could have been present, and their mere existence would put a person's mind at ease. After all, they were heroes. They would never do something nefarious against their own kind.

Cassie was safe. She decided to prod the leader by asking him a lingering question, "Sorry if this comes across as rude, but why are you here?"

It was a reasonable question. Most people assumed the commanders were off enjoying a lush retirement. A life free from any more turmoil was the least that they deserved after orchestrating such a grand event. Unfortunately, that was only a belief. No one could confirm it because the commander's identities remained hidden. Only those directly involved with the night from twenty years ago knew the truth, but even their knowledge was limited. The few scraps of information that were available were tightly held onto and rarely exposed.

"With a goal as lofty as ours, a strong leader is needed. I felt that I was the best person to fill that role out of the three remaining commanders," Tartarus said before his voice trailed off. The room's temperature noticeably dropped. A grim atmosphere loomed. Respect kept the three from speaking, and shock forced Cassie to remain silent. No one knew how to respond. Tartarus was giving Cassie a chance to speak.

Her morbid curiosity eventually took the bait. "Sir, you don't mean… Which of the commanders passed away?" Cassie asked with a nervous voice.

The subject was clearly sensitive. Not even his unique mask could hide the sorrow Tartarus felt. It was always rumored that the commanders were close friends that kept in contact with each other, and Tartarus's current demeanor proved that to be accurate. Cassie felt as if she stepped on a landmine. She didn't mean to dig up old memories, but her curiosity had gotten the better of her. Knowledge of the commander's private lives was nonexistent. The sudden reveal that two were deceased would shock anyone.

"It was Nyx and Erebus. The commanders of the Mobile and Armored Battalions respectively," Tartarus said. He bowed his head in respect for his fallen friends. They were the closest things he ever had to a family. The two were practically his brother and sister. It was why he was reluctant to talk about their death to Cassie in this way.

"I'm sorry for your loss," Cassie said. She had never felt more deflated. As a mobile-type Evolved, she resonated with Nyx and idolized her. She even dreamed about getting to meet her hero someday and receiving an autograph.

It was nauseating to hear that her type's commander passed away unceremoniously. The two commanders deserved a grand send-off. A public funeral would have been less ideal but satisfying nonetheless. Unfortunately, such an event would go against the commander's desired secrecy and negatively affect their families.

"No, I'm sorry," Tartarus said quietly. It may have been better to avoid this topic, but he wanted to tell his guest a portion of the truth. He didn't mean for it to ruin the mood. The conversation needed to be reined in before its purpose was lost on grievances. Thankfully, Tartarus wasn't the only person who could shift to the next topic.

"We'd prefer if you refrain from revealing this information to anyone. Alright, hon? Knowing that they're dead reduces the list of potential suspects for any would-be detectives," Hemera said, breaking the awkward tension. Her request didn't need to be said. This kind of knowledge could spur people to start asking questions about who the commanders were. Plenty of humans also wanted that information for prosecution purposes. Hemera pressed forward and answered one of Cassie's remaining questions. "Back on track, we would like to offer you a temporary position on our team. Your assets would greatly assist us with monitoring the Primal during tonight's operation.

Cassie immediately froze. Hemera's words echoed in her mind. Conflict set in. Cassie had just met one of the heroes her father would tell about during his late-night stories. Now, that same hero wanted to work with her. There should have been no question in her mind. Any Evolved would be over the moon for such an invitation, yet Cassie couldn't respond positively. After such a horrifying night, she couldn't accept the offer.

"I...don't...know..." Cassie said slowly. It was difficult to outright refuse the offer. Tartarus should have already known her condition. Their initial encounter may have been brief, but the facts were obvious. Primals terrified Cassie. The same was true for Fallen but to a lesser extent. Of course, she wasn't the only person to feel this way. Plenty of Evolved feared Primals and Fallen. Most people with non-combative abilities avoided them at all costs and dreaded the possibility of encountering one. Cassie's phobia in particular was etched into her at an early age and reinforced recently.

"Guess the boss wasn't lying when he said you freak out over Primals. Sucks to be you. But, hey, look on the bright side. You're the first person to ever reject his recruitment offer," Nike said as she leaned back in her chair.

Her mocking attitude would have irritated Cassie if the conversation was about anything else. She couldn't argue with what was said. Nike was free to say whatever rude thought popped into her head. Thankfully, she was interrupted before any more passive-aggressive insults were hurled.

"To an extent, I can understand your fears. I've seen many of my friends succumb to this blight," Tartarus said. He nodded his head in solidarity.

Everyone, even someone as powerful as him, had some type of horror story involving either Fallen or Primals. The only difference was how the person reacted and grew from the experience. The Celestials opted to better themselves and aimed to resolve the looming threat. Meanwhile, Cassie was left shattered and forced to collect the pieces alone following her mother's passing.

Tartarus continued his grandiose proclamation. "But that is the reason why we exist. We aim to solve both the Fallen and Primal dilemmas, so the next generation will not have to."

⁘⸱⦂⸱⦂⸱⁘

The Celestials took great pride in their work. Everyone showed up to meetings on time. Tasks were done without complaint. Rooms were kept spotless, minus the individual quarters provided to each member. The group acted much better than a simple rogue team of Evolved. Even so, it was still alarming to see them all together in one place. Each member was powerful in their own right and critical to the team. Cassie felt overwhelmed simply sitting at the same table as them. She wasn't used to sharing a room with people like this, or never noticed if she did. What made the scenario worse was how casual the Celestials were.

"Nice to meet 'cha. I'm Iris." The woman wearing the geometrical mask and abstract suit said. There was no discernible hierarchy aside from the commander and team leaders, so she spoke first simply out of excitement.

Much like Hemera and Nike, the newcomers had their voices altered to prevent potential recognition. That didn't stop Iris from trying her best to sound friendly. The smile could be heard through her words alone, but Cassie felt uneasy about the warm greeting. Iris was the one that prevented her from escaping, and Cassie sliced Iris's arm with an AE knife. They should have every reason to hate each other but didn't. The same wasn't true for everyone.

"Thanatos," the skull-masked man said bluntly. He kept his arms folded as if he was irritated that Cassie was still around. The prior night had little effect on him personally, but he continued to be visibly upset. His cold introduction was met with a quiet sigh from Hemera. She probably hoped that the group would refrain from scaring their guest. There was no reason to further sully their name and reputation with an outsider by being rude. At least, that was what Cassie assumed.

"Yo, I'm Hypnos. Don't mind the sour puss. He's just upset that a noob got the better of him," the newly introduced member said. The young man was likely close to Cassie's age. He wore a light gray suit with a matching vest and tie. A sweatshirt sat snuggly underneath, bulking his figure and keeping him warm. The hood was pulled over his head for concealment, and a spiked leather mask covered his nose and mouth. Soft eyewear with large 'X's over the eyes blinded Hypnos and veiled the rest of his face. Finally, black nylon was worn just in case his hood ever fell.

Hypnos raised his hand to give a polite wave but flinched when his arm reached a certain height. He tried to casually hide the pain he felt but to no avail. It was painfully obvious that he had some type of shoulder injury. Given his line of work, that was to be expected. Cassie was somewhat alarmed that his injury was severe enough to last until morning. She wanted to ask about it, but the introductions went on.

The final two masked men spoke. "We are Gemini. The ones that caught you last night. Sorry for the roughness, but you're too fast." They looked at each other for a moment. A silent debate raged before the two broke their mirrored stare. Who would speak first was somehow decided despite the lack of verbal communication. One watched Cassie while the other looked down to prevent confusion over who was speaking.

"I am Pollux, brother of Castor," the first man said. His traditional comedy mask matched the glee in his voice. A wide grin and cheerful eyes were stark contrasts from their ivory base. The openings were layered with a black film to prevent revealing any of the man's features, and it gave the mask a uniquely flat appearance. His interesting suit was vertically split with the right consisting of a vibrant red and the left an alluring black. A knitted crimson heart was etched atop his chest pocket which stood out against the void-like material.

"I am Castor, brother of Pollux," the other man said with a quieter voice. His head shot up while his brother's tilted down, revealing a traditional tragedy mask. A looming frown covered his mouth and depressed eyes looked forward. It was unclear if the mask represented the wearer's current emotion like Pollux's did. Following the trend of opposites, Castor's suit was the inverted version of his brother, and a black spade replaced the heart that would have been over his crimson pocket.

The two rose from their seats and stepped back from the central table. In an act of good faith, they decided to reveal their Armaments. Pollux held a hand near his face. Ichor swarmed the glove he wore, stretching to the end of his fingers to form dagger-like claws. The dark matter hardened and formed sleek edges that swept through the air. Droplets of a clear liquid formed along his claws, no doubt some type of poison. This refined weapon was interesting to look at, but it quickly took action. In a single strike, Pollux sliced through his other arm.

The cut was deep and gruesome, to the point that bone could be seen. Cassie was the only person to flinch while the others grimaced. She closed her eyes and looked away. Several seconds had to pass for her to regain her courage to look once again. Her eyes widened when she noticed that most of the gash was gone. The laceration had automatically closed itself thanks to Pollux's hyper regeneration. It took less than a minute for the grave injury to revert to its normal state.

Castor didn't allow his brother to hold the spotlight for long. He held up his arm and clenched his fist. Ichor covered his arm and hand, forming several layers before hardening. The resulting bulked formation could even be seen through his jacket. Pollux turned and swiped at his brother without the slightest bit of hesitation. The claws that once tore through his own flesh scraped against Castor's arm. A shrill metallic sound rang through the room as the two objects clashed. Part of the suit was shredded from the display, but it swiftly repaired itself. Not only did Castor prove his defenses were admirable, but he also managed to showcase the impressive uniform he wore. Both men turned to Cassie once the performance had ended.

"Uh, cool?" Cassie said, not sure how to respond.

The brothers' act was appreciated but unnecessarily gruesome and theatrical. A simple gesture would have sufficed. It also would have been much less horrifying. Every other member of the group ignored the odd duo and returned their attention to the table. This wasn't the first time they'd seen the performance, and it was likely not going to be the last either.

"Told you we should have done a flip," Pollux said.

The two men were the only Celestials to plan their introductions. They wanted to welcome Cassie while showing off their Armaments. It was certainly memorable but not in the way they would have preferred. The guest of honor was more concerned than ever before. Pollux continued to mumble to himself as he sat in his chair, and Castor mirrored his brother's movements perfectly.

"Now that introductions are over, the meeting can finally commence," Tartarus said with an authoritative voice. "First order of business, Cassie's temporary admittance into the Celestials so that she may assist us in locating the Primal." Everyone else remained quiet out of respect for the leader, so he paused and allowed them to speak. Two hands shot up immediately in protest.

"I object," Nike and Thanatos said in unison. The two looked at each other, surprised by the coincidence.

Tartarus's proclamations rarely received opposition. He spent a great amount of time mulling over each point before presenting them in the group's meeting. That didn't mean objections were unwelcome, but a counter-argument had to be made against the commander. Otherwise, the opposition was simply wasting its time.

"According to your report, sir, the girl is petrified by Primals. She even played dead when one got close rather than exploiting its lack of mobile-type Armament. This shows that she lacks confidence and experience," Thanatos said.

His argument was so sound that even Cassie found herself agreeing with it. As expected, Tartarus told the Celestials about the encounter in great detail. Each member formed their own opinions about Cassie and how valuable she was to the team. Some believed her assistance would expedite the Primal search. Others knew the disadvantages of involving a scared civilian.

"I agree," Nike said. "Though she totally got the better of almost half our team, that won't translate well when it comes to actual combat against a Primal. Some of us are dunces, but I can't say we're as mindless and unpredictable as our target."

Nike chuckled, fondly remembering listening to the report of the previous night's antics. At first, she seethed with anger over Iris's injury, but the memory became much more entertaining with time. Hemera was followed back to headquarters. Thanatos was tricked by a rogue arrowhead that was thrown on a whim. Iris failed to properly restrain her opponent. Even the Gemini brothers would have been duped had they not surprised Cassie.

"If I may, sir, I don't think I'd be a good addition to the team, either. Even in a temporary position, I can't handle Primals. I'm sorry," Cassie said.

It hurt to turn down a request from such an esteemed person, but her fear was an undeniable fact. She gave a silent thanks to the two that spoke against the idea. It would have been nice if they were a little less blunt, but any help was appreciated. Although, the decision was far from one-sided.

"It is true that Cassiopeia lacks the mental fortitude to engage in direct combat with Primals. That said, she only needs to act as a scout and decoy. Try to think of yourself as a highly advanced drone designed to track targets and pester enemies. Not as scary, is it?" Tartarus said, trying his best to win over those that stood against him.

Cassie wasn't keen on the idea of being compared to an inanimate object, but the situation did become less daunting. She could fly out of the Primal's reach and perform reconnaissance. Then, there were the benefits of joining to consider.

"Come on, boss. I think our little birdy needs a bit more of an incentive. No one likes working for free," Pollux said. He casually gazed at the claw he formed which tapped along the table while his other unaltered hand swiped through his tablet.

What he suggested wasn't unordinary. Members of the group could only operate under their own sense of justice for so long. Payments and prizes were necessary to keep a person motivated.

"I concur. How about a free dinner in the Yellow Zone? One close to the Green Zone, of course. Maybe you'd like a vintage bottle of liquor? Or would you prefer straight cash? We could even handle your college tuition if that's your price," Castor said, joining his brother in sweetening the pot.

No one objected to the offers, so the rewards must have been feasible to give. The only issue was how good it all sounded. It felt like making a deal with the devil.

Cassie gulped. The negotiations had taken a turn. She wanted nothing more than to leave without committing to anything but offers like these didn't come every day. Her family was low on funds. Taking advantage of the situation could benefit more than just herself. The financial stress that Leo and Lyra faced would be alleviated albeit slightly. Orion could quit his part-time job, and Cassie would be praised as a savior to the siblings. Then again, high-class Yellow Zone restaurants were nothing to scoff at. It was an alluring thought, but Cassie quickly chased it away. Family came first.

"Oh, I know! How about a motorcycle? Something nice and sleek for you to drive around once the Anti-Armament law gets enforced. You won't be able to fly around for long. Why not start preparing for it now?" Pollux said.

Within a few months, it would be illegal for an Evolved to use their Armament freely. The very idea was ridiculous. Humans tried to justify the law by associating it with various gun control laws, but there was still heavy opposition. Politics aside, Cassie's wings would soon be clipped. Occurrences like the one with Enforcer Romeo would become all the more prevalent.

"It's better than a car. You could store it almost anywhere, even in a small house. If you can't hide it, you could always sell it," Iris said, adding more positives to her friend's proposal.

She wasn't entirely wrong about the storage issue. The Red Zone was incredibly congested, and the same was true for Cassie's garage. It was already at max capacity with the surplus of items her deceased parents left behind. A motorcycle was the only vehicle that could fit without disturbing much of the memories that lingered in that garage.

"Something tells me she wouldn't outright sell it," Hemera said. She was able to accurately read Cassie like a book. The young woman would never sell such a kind gift, especially not in these trying times. Cassie would gain more from keeping the motorcycle than selling it. Arguments with her siblings over who got car privileges would be null and void for her. She'd never have to consult with them over appointments and schedules. She could earn the freedom she always wanted.

"Wait, why didn't I get these kinds of offers when I joined?" Hypnos asked. He threw up his arms in protest only to immediately wince in pain. His wounded shoulder still stung, but he would never openly admit it. Ridicule and harassment were all he would get from this group. Although, as the newest member of the Celestials, that would happen regardless.

"Dude, you stumbled through our door looking to join us. We actually need her," Nike said.

Her uncaring and brutal tone made the statement hit even harder. While the order of member recruitment wasn't clear, Hypnos was undeniably the newest member. He was friends with everyone present, but there was a distinct lack of mutual respect. He likely hadn't proved himself on any missions yet, and his injured shoulder certainly didn't boost the group's confidence in him. Vicious mockery always hounded recruits in any profession, and Nike seemed to excel in this particular craft.

"Good one!" Thanatos chuckled. He had stayed relatively silent for long enough that Cassie nearly forgot about him. His arms were still crossed like a belligerent child. His objection had fallen on deaf ears which bothered him beyond belief. Nike, who was aligned with him, had already moved on. She wasn't the type to hold grudges, and Thanatos was no different. It didn't take much longer for his sour shell to crack. Cassie's potential admittance to the group suddenly didn't seem as bad.

With all of the chaos going on, Cassie was lost in the moment. She wanted to voice her opinion, but it was hard to interrupt this group of chattering friends. Thankfully, Tartarus was present and acted as the only adult in the room. He shut down the disturbance before it got any worse. He cleared his throat and the discussion ended. Everyone fell to a hush. Their gazes returned to Cassie, who had yet to respond to a single offer.

"I'm sorry. I can't possibly make a decision right now," Cassie said with a low voice. She needed reasonable and unbiased people to converse with. Most of the Celestials were eager for her to join, but that didn't make the position any less dangerous. Cassie knew it wouldn't be right to risk her life without the consent of her family. She couldn't possibly do that.

"That's understandable. I didn't expect you to give me an immediate answer," Tartarus said with a polite nod. "Take the day to mull it over, but tell no one about what you've seen or heard here."

⠏⠗⠊⠝⠉⠑

"Watch your head," Castor said as he assisted Cassie into the back of a pickup truck. Its unnecessarily large tires made it difficult to enter without a running start, and its revving engine made it seem eager to leave. Pollux bounced in the driver's seat as he waited for the others to get ready. Cassie tried to argue that she could return home alone. She thought it was best if the Celestials didn't know where she lived, but Tartarus insisted otherwise. He gave Gemini the order to escort her home, much to the dismay of all three involved.

The white truck was the only vehicle that sat outside of the apartment complex. Everyone aside from the three decided to remain in the building until their guest left. They had more to discuss about the upcoming mission, and they wanted to leave without the worry of being followed. Gemini would have to get the debrief from their team leader later. In the meantime, some questions still needed to be asked.

"So, like, are you guys actually brothers? Or is that just a bit?" Cassie asked in a joking manner. She sat back in her seat and stared ahead. A thin wall separated her from the front two seats. It seemed recently installed for the sole purpose of hiding the driver's identity while they drove without a mask. Cassie would have preferred to have a normal conversation, but that was clearly out of the question. She was forced to ask whatever was on her mind and hope Gemini would answer. Unfortunately, they had yet to give a response. Cassie knocked against the thin barrier and repeated her question.

Again, she only received silence. It was obvious that no amount of pestering would get her an answer. Even Pollux, who seemed to be the most talkative person, was silent. Cassie was left with no one to converse with. The rumbling engine provided excellent background noise as she explored her thoughts. Meanwhile, the truck drove on without direction. Cassie was concerned with how Gemini knew where she lived, but those worries diminished almost immediately. The Celestials likely found out where she lived via her personal belongings and internet research.

Cassie found it better to worry about the most pressing issue: whether she would accept Tartarus's offer. She could risk her life and become a Celestial, or she could remain in her normal civilian life. Her gift of flight could be used to find and fight Primals, or it could be used as a simple means of transportation. The duality of both sides of this decision was what made it intense. Cassie wasn't sure if she was ready to take that leap of faith.

Alright, Cassie. Deep breath. Let's take this one step at a time. First, what are the benefits? Cassie thought to herself. The most prominent benefit was the reward she'd receive. None of the Celestials argued against the proposed prizes, so they were all up for the taking. What she wanted exactly was still being debated. Reducing her family's financial struggles by taking the cash or paying college tuition seemed to be the best choice, but the more selfish options were also tantalizing.

Of course, some benefits took place outside of Cassie's personal scope. Eradicating the roaming Primal would save many lives. The loftier goal of potentially ending this crisis could change the world, and it would prevent people like Cassie from growing up in fear. The Celestials would be regarded as heroes, etched in history alongside the commanders of the Night of A Thousand Blades. Cassie had the chance of being a part of something bigger than herself.

But, am I really that noble of a person? Cassie thought. She always believed the famous five commanders had unbreakable will and passion that yearned for a better world. If that was the case, she was far from being like them. She was afraid of the sacrifice it would take to be like them. She didn't want to risk losing the people she loved because she overstepped her boundaries. Most of all, Cassie was terrified of dying. The thought that her family would never know the truth made the idea even worse. She could never do that to them.

She could never betray their trust.

Trust... They have a lot of trust in someone they know nothing about... Cassie's thoughts echoed for a moment. A question popped into her mind that bothered her to no end. Why did the Celestials trust Cassie so much? They allowed her to leave their base of operations. They let her participate in a meeting and offered her a spot on the team. Finally, they told her about the death of two commanders. It was the last part that perplexed Cassie the most. Tartarus had no reason to reveal that information. If he truly wanted to protect Nyx's and Erebus's identities, he should have avoided the topic entirely by giving a vague answer.

That wasn't the only issue with the present commander. A level of secrecy surrounded the Celestials. They all wore masks and went to great lengths to conceal themselves. Codenames were used to avoid identification, and even voice modulators were frequently utilized. Tartarus was the only person to neglect such a feature. His voice remained unaltered as if he was the only person in the room who wasn't afraid of being exposed. Cassie laughed at the thought. Polus was far too big of a city for her to know all of the Celestials. If anything, she knew one of them but that was a fleeting guess with limited evidence.

There were certainly silhouettes that matched those of her friends, but it could be nothing more than a coincidence. Her friends and family were of average height and physique. Most of their Armaments were rather generic as well. Cassie couldn't imagine the number of people who had claws or extendable limbs within the city. Assault-types and mobile-types were predictable in that regard. The same was true for Castor's boring armor, leaving only Nike to prominently stand out with her invisibility.

Wait... Claws, armor, whips, and camo. That's not all of them, right? Cassie thought. She racked her brain trying to think of the past few hours. Each Evolved had an Armament, so Cassie should have counted eight from her night away from home. She combed through her memories for even the slightest hint. She had to know what the three Armaments were. There was no way she had forgotten about them. Those three Celestials must have exposed themselves at some point. If they hadn't, then why?

Cassie grew cold for a moment. The idea that plagued her mind was ridiculous. She almost laughed at the thought. The evidence was far too circumstantial. It was like aimlessly throwing a dart through a dark room and hoping to hit something. Was it possible? Sure. All it took was an incredible amount of coincidences coupled with extreme luck. The chance of that singular idea being real was pitifully small, yet it occupied Cassie's entire train of thought.

She could almost hear the click in her mind when it all came together. There was evidence. Bits and pieces that alone meant nothing but together revealed everything. It all made sense. Hiding a lie was easier when you had accomplices. Simple stories could be spun into well-crafted alibis with enough effort and false witnesses. The only question now was how Cassie planned to expose the truth. If she failed, future attempts would only be more difficult. This had to be done perfectly.

Suddenly, the truck came to a complete stop without warning. Cassie's body shifted forward, almost colliding with the wall. She would have been upset if she had the energy. Instead, most of her focus was on her thoughts. The warm sensation within her heart was faltering. It was replaced with a lingering frost that showed no mercy. This wasn't the time for doubts, yet she wasn't sure if it was right to reveal everything. After all, Tartarus asked her not to do that.

"Here we are. Home sweet home," Pollux said with glee. His voice was altered, but it was obvious that he was happy to talk again. It must have been grueling for him to remain silent. Driving with a mask on would have aroused suspicion, so he kept it off and was forced to leave his modified voice alongside it. The Gemini brothers had likely re-equipped themselves to prevent Cassie from peeking at them.

In reality, that was the last thing on her mind. She had a mission of her own to complete that required her full attention. The identity of those odd men could be revealed later. They were eager to leave, unhappy that they got stuck with a tedious escort mission. They also probably had lives to return to.

"Take it easy. Try not to stress about your decision," Castor said with a low voice. Even with an altered voice, his words were sincere. It was almost as if he truly cared about Cassie. She would have replied in kind, but her mind was occupied. The plan she developed still needed work. A confession wouldn't come easily.

Cassie hopped out of the truck, stumbling on her way out due to its height. She checked for her belongings one final time. Everything had been returned to her without question, although Nike was wary of returning the AE knife. The heavy truck door slammed shut with the slightest push, and Pollux was quick to gripe about treating his vehicle with more respect. Castor waved it off and demanded they take the backroads to avoid traffic. Their friendly banter continued, but Cassie ignored most of it.

She took a deep breath before turning to face the wooden door she'd known for many years.

Where did all of that time go? Cassie thought. It seemed like just yesterday she was posing for a family photo. The yard she stood in hosted many fights with her brothers and sister throughout the years. They were simpler times. An era where there were no worries. Cassie yearned for those days to return, but they were long gone. She had to face reality.

A new sensation formed within Cassie, one that she hadn't felt in a long time. Emptiness. This hollow feeling grew within her chest. Hope was dissipating. She clung to the thought that she was wrong. If she was, she could deny the Celestials and everything would go back to normal. However, if she was right about her hunch, her world would soon be turned on its head. The door that separated her from the others never seemed more intimidating. The looming dread suffocated her. A mess of emotions swirled within her. She could have waited on that porch for hours, but that wasn't an option.

Cassie reached for the doorknob that separated her from her fate. She readied herself for war. This argument was not going to be easy.

Then, her hand stopped. It wasn't from the terror she felt. No, she was used to being afraid at this point. This was a different feeling. Curiosity. There was a noticeably missing sensation that she should be feeling. The front door was rather barren. She narrowed her eyes to better her vision, but there wasn't enough time to analyze the situation.

The front door swung open. Cassie recoiled from the sudden motion. She took several steps back, but something stopped her. A rope made of ichor reached from within the house to grip Cassie. Emma emerged from the dark interior, holding the product of her Armament with a tight grip. Her aura was dark and intimidating. The pressure that came from her was nauseating. She was beyond enraged, though her face remained unchanged. Cassie immediately got flashbacks to her days as a child, but she had never angered her aunt to this extent.

"Right on time. We need to talk," Emma said before sending out more ichor webs. She pulled her niece into the house without mercy and glared at the truck Gemini sat in. The two brothers looked at each other. They yelled something inaudible out of panic and sped away. The last thing they wanted was to be involved in whatever was about to happen.

Chapter 5: Flare

"Well well well. Look who finally decided to show up! Do you have any idea how worried we were?!" Leo shouted, starting his lecture. He and Lyra paced around the kitchen as they took turns yelling at Cassie, who hadn't said a word since she arrived.

Emma quietly sat by the back door and watched the show. Meanwhile, Orion was left to oddly stand in the hallway and remain quiet. It wasn't his turn to be lectured for losing Cassie.

"Sweetie, what are we supposed to do with you? We agreed that you wouldn't go out there. Why can't you two just be good students and keep your heads down?" Lyra said with a much calmer voice compared to Leo's. At this point, she vented out her frustration over everything.

The younger two weren't as obedient as they should have been. They didn't realize their roles. Then, there was their estranged aunt that always caused trouble.

"The agreement stated that you all stayed," Emma blankly said. She didn't waste a second to remind the group that they were all at fault. Despite their best efforts and reasonings, the twins were no better than their younger counterparts. Cassie's only problem was that she returned late. The confrontation would have been reversed had she come home as planned.

"Now's not the time for that," Leo replied with a much calmer voice. He was reasonable enough to refrain from shouting at his aunt. Or rather, he knew what would happen if he angered her further. He likely would have been tied and strung from the ceiling. The image somewhat haunted him. His and Lyra's actions from the previous night had gone unpunished. It was only a matter of time before they got their comeuppance.

"Cassie, we were worried about you. They're not good at showing it, but they care." Orion chimed into the conversation. He walked over to comfort his little sister. Gentle hands rubbed her shoulders as he tried to ease her tension. The attempt might have worked if Cassie was afraid or nervous. Instead, it had the opposite effect and only fueled her frustration.

Cassie shot up from her seat and swatted her brother's hand away. As she turned to face him, a swift hand grabbed his shoulder. Cassie smiled sweetly, but her menacing nature seeped through the facade. Something inside her snapped. Reasoning with the others, while they were in this state, was impossible. She needed to make a stand. One that halted her siblings' momentum and gave her an opening to attack. Thankfully, Orion was the perfect subject to enact this plan. Cassie strengthened her grip on her brother's shoulder, causing him to wince in pain. The previous night's fight left him sore, so this pressure felt worse than ever before.

"What's the matter, Hypnos? Forget to drink your Nectar?" Cassie said with a shaking voice. The cold glare she gave her brother was unlike anything she'd ever shown before. Her grip tightened as if she was trying to squeeze the answer out of him. The others were shocked by the scene before them. Leo and Lyra never would have imagined that their sister would act out so violently, and Emma was intrigued by the sudden role reversal.

"No, I just forgot after…what…happened…" Orion's voice trailed off. The words Cassie said finally reached him. His pale face somehow got even whiter. He didn't know what to say. His mind raced for an answer that would never come. He glanced at the others, but they all stared at him. They were practically waiting at the edge of their seats for his response.

The words were caught in his throat, but Cassie gave no time for a proper response. She got her answer from his hesitation. Now, there were two more to investigate. She shoved her brother away, forcing him to stumble into Leo. The two fell from the unexpected attack while Emma and Lyra watched with disappointed expressions. Lyra immediately stepped forward to quell her sister's tantrum, but a large wing spontaneously filled her vision and swept her off her feet. Cassie retracted her wing and faced her defeated siblings.

"I'm disappointed. The Celestials seemed like a strong group, but you three got your butts kicked by me. Tartarus would be disappointed, huh?" Cassie said with a mocking tone. She had never felt this fulfilled. Never before had she beaten all of her siblings in combat. Their frantic response must have been linked to the confrontational topic. Her thoughts raced for the perfect strategy. Two more confessions were needed, but they would have to come from the most stubborn people she knew.

"Interesting. Elaborate," Emma said, demanding an explanation for Cassie's bold claim. She had already shown subtle irritation toward Tartarus's name, so the mention of him agitated her. Even with her annoyance, she had yet to show any signs of allegiance to one particular party. She wasn't making any moves to support anyone. Instead, Emma decided to play the role of arbiter. She placed herself between the opposing parties and waited for the debate to commence.

"They're Celestials. The group that Tartarus is leading. The same group that abducted me last night. I would've come back if they didn't snatch me out of the sky," Cassie said, continuing her accusation. She wanted to shout her words from the rooftops. Betrayal and anger festered within her, and she was eager to let it all out. Of course, proper indictments required proof of wrong-doing.

"I hope you have evidence," Emma said. She cocked her head to the side and watched her belligerent niece. From her point of view, this accusation came out of nowhere. Her morning was supposed to be spent disciplining the children. They all disobeyed her by leaving. Even Orion was guilty. Emma thought she would swiftly dispense their punishments and return home, but that fantasy would have to wait for another time. For now, she had to see if and why her charges were prancing around the city at night with masks on.

"Only three of them refused to show me their Armaments. Co-incidentally, they had the same basic features as these three idiots," Cassie said with confidence. True, the evidence was extremely bare and circumstantial, but one couldn't deny the similarities. Hypnos had a wounded shoulder which matched Orion. Hemera was kind and spoke in the same manner Lyra did. Then, there was Thanatos who was a prick, much like Leo. Cassie could see the connections, especially on that last point.

"That's all you got? Really? And that's somehow proof that we're members of some cult?" Leo said with a condescending tone. His younger sister was clearly having a hard time. She had spent the past few days struggling and in fear. An encounter with a Primal would be exciting enough, but meeting a strange group led by a former battalion commander was pushing Cassie to her limits. It was no wonder why she was spouting nonsense.

"Well, you're definitely not Nike, Iris, or Gemini," Cassie said. She didn't mean to bring up the other masked people. This was a trial involving her three siblings. She could worry about the remaining four members later. Cassie took a deep breath. She needed to calm herself before she accidentally ruined her only chance.

"Now you're just saying names from mythology," Lyra responded. She played with the pendant that hung around her neck. It hurt her to alienate her sister. This would undoubtedly divide the family even further. Even so, Lyra assumed the role of a proxy mother. She had to be stern during these trying times. Such a sentiment was easier said than done.

"Irrelevant. Get back to how they are Celestials," Emma said. The conversation was getting sidetracked. She needed to reign it in before the group got lost down a web of conspiracies.

"Yeah. Out of all the people in Polus, why do you think we'd be a part of those eight people?" Leo said with a confident smile. Cassie was out of her mind if she thought she could perfectly accuse her siblings. Polus was an impressively sized city with a considerable Evolved population. Any one of them could be the questionable three masked individuals that Cassie was focused on. She needed more proof. Thankfully, Leo had given her what she wanted.

"Eight? Why would you be a part of those *eight* people?" Cassie said. That number echoed in her mind. Finally, she found the smoking gun. There was no denying what he said and what it implied. Accomplishment welled within, but fear did as well. If she won against her siblings like she always wanted to, the betrayal would be solidified. It would be proven that her brothers and sister had been acting out and risking their lives. Even so, Cassie pressed on with the linchpin of her argument. "Leo, how did you know there were eight of them?"

"Sweetie, you named all eight of them. It's not hard to do the math," Lyra said. She seemed perplexed by the odd question. Cassie was accusing them of being three members of the Celestials. She named the remaining members, and Tartarus was automatically included in the count. A child could count the names that were given. So, why was Cassie making such a big fuss? That answer was rather simple. So simple, in fact, that almost everyone overlooked it.

"That'd be true. If you knew Gemini was two people."

"Well-" Lyra tried to respond but her words got caught in her throat.

She didn't know what to say. Leo was no better. The two stood with astonished expressions. They looked like a pair of fish out of water, gasping for air and frantically looking for a solution to their plight. Orion also tried to think of a way out, but nothing came to mind. Only Emma was able to continue the conversation.

"It is a large leap for simple speculation. Leo. Lyra. Care to explain how you know that Gemini consists of both Castor and Pollux?" Emma asked. She turned to face the bewildered children. Her quizzical expression was reflected back at her. Neither sibling had an answer, but they were more than willing to divert the conversation. Even if it meant feeding their aunt to the wolves.

"Oh yeah? How do you know that the brothers are named Castor and Pollux? Seems like you could explain yourself a bit more too," Leo said. He needed to deflect attention from himself and his twin sister. Venom doused his words, but Emma paid them no mind. She wasn't the least bit interested in participating in a circular argument.

"Aunt Emma, we-" Orion tried to offer a better explanation that was less critical. Unfortunately, his words were cut off. There was no room for excuses.

"Irrelevant. You all got caught. By the one you deemed inferior," Emma said with a stern voice. Her eyes stared coldly at the three who veiled themselves with lies and deceit. Leo, Lyra, and Orion exchanged glances. No amount of diversions would distract from the truth that was revealed. The battle was over, and the victor was plain to see.

"So, I'm right?" Cassie asked. She felt conflicted. Part of her wanted to celebrate the accomplishment of winning against all of her siblings, but that was coupled with anguish and stress. Her question was the last chance to wipe everything away. The three could find another excuse. They could deny all that was said. The four could return to their old lives. Unfortunately, that was no longer an option. Cassie had dug her grave and needed to lie in it.

"You are. Congratulations," Emma said with a few unenthusiastic claps. She was proud to see how far the youngest child had grown, although she didn't express it. Fond memories of the constantly crying girl appeared in her mind. She wondered if this was what all parents felt when they looked at their grown children, but now was not the time to reminisce. Her other three charges had yet to confess.

"No, I want to hear it from them," Cassie demanded. She wasn't sure if she could maintain her composure after hearing the truth, but she wanted her siblings to be the ones that explained everything. From their motives to their secrecy, she had to know it all.

The heavy atmosphere loomed as Leo, Lyra, and Orion hesitated. None of them were sure what the proper procedure was. The three had sworn themselves to secrecy. Confessing would essentially be them betraying the Celestials and, worst of all, Tartarus. They would have preferred to stay quiet, but they knew better than to do that. It was difficult to disobey direct orders from their commander, so the next highest-ranking Celestial decided to set an example for the others.

"You're right, sweetheart. It's the least you deserve. So, hello, I am Hemera. Alpha Team Leader of the Celestials," Lyra said with a soft voice. She was ashamed to have been caught, but there were few options. As a team leader, she excused the reveal as a necessity. Her formal bow to Cassie was a signal to the others. She would take responsibility for the inevitable repercussions.

"Hypnos here, but you already knew that. I'm the newest member of the Celestials, which is probably why I made such a simple mistake," Orion said. He rubbed the back of his head and let out a defeated sigh. He knew no one blamed him, but that didn't make the failure sting any less. His injured shoulder likely tipped Cassie off to her initial suspicions. From there, it was only a matter of time until she figured everything out. That was why he wanted to take the fall alone.

"Thanatos," Leo said. He crossed his arms and avoided eye contact.

It was almost a perfect recreation of his introduction from earlier that morning. He hated how things turned out, but it was too late to change anything. Cassie was the last person he wanted to know about the Celestials. It would have been best for her to remain ignorant of the family's after-hours activities. It would have saved her the heartache.

⁘ ⁙ ⁖ ⁙ ⁘

"Why?" Cassie asked as tears formed in her eyes. Not even the word *betrayed* could encompass how she felt. How much of it was a lie? When did it all start? The family's disorderly schedule helped mask what the three were doing. Anyone could easily slip away and blame external circumstances. Cassie's mind generated hypothetical situations where her siblings lied about their actions. It hurt to know they didn't trust her with that information, so she wanted to know their reasoning above all else.

"We want to help end the-" Leo started.

"Cut it out! Give me the real answer, damn you!" Cassie yelled. She marched over to Leo and grabbed his shirt. She was beyond tired of all the excuses and dancing around the topic. The lie was obvious. None of her siblings were altruistic enough to operate in that line of work for free. They certainly weren't the type to want their names written in history books. In reality, they had no reason to join the Celestials. Cassie made sure to point that out. "We're not the heroes of some story! We're orphans that can barely get by with the money we make! So, why do something so dangerous?!"

"We're...continuing...dad's legacy..." Lyra mumbled. Her words were close to silent. Almost to the point that no one heard them. She didn't feel guilty over what was said. Instead, what she felt was more akin to embarrassment. What she said was no different than a child earnestly admitting they'd accomplish some impossible goal. As an adult, Lyra didn't like to admit her lofty goal, and she certainly didn't want to explain it in detail.

"What?" Cassie said with a confused expression. Their father had been dead for quite some time. If any project of his was still standing, it'd be covered in dust and lost somewhere in the garage. Orion Sr. had his fair share of crafts, but he wasn't the type of man to involve himself in guerrilla warfare against Primals. At least, not the father that Cassie remembered.

"Dad was-" Orion tried to say.

"Irrelevant. Cassie requested your purpose. Why join the Celestials?" Emma interrupted the conversation. She clearly knew more than she was letting on but wouldn't divulge her secrets. Emma decided that the conversation was better directed at the siblings' reasoning rather than anything else, and it was hard to argue against her. Once she set her mind to something, it was next to impossible to sway her.

"Lyra and I joined after hearing about dad's role in its formation. We wanted to be a part of what he created, to solve the problem that tore our lives to shreds. It just sucks that we couldn't work alongside him." Leo said, finally answering the question. He rubbed his silver watch and gazed at the floor. It was surprising to hear about how their father formed such a group. Even as an armor-type Evolved, Orion Sr. often avoided conflict whenever necessary. It was hard to believe such a kind-hearted man would purposefully fight against Primals in secret, but Cassie was quickly learning that everyone held their cards close to their chest.

"I got wrapped up in it a few months ago when I followed them like you did," Orion said with a slight grin. It was obvious that his alternative persona, Hypnos, was new to the group. Even so, Cassie never would have guessed he joined so recently. Nothing changed from his day-to-day life that would have clued her into the truth. So, these three had some sort of system in place to operate as Celestials while keeping Cassie in the dark.

"Why didn't you tell me?" Cassie asked. Her anger had subsided and was replaced with grief. Although, the feeling didn't last long. Betrayal lingered in her mind, but it diminished with each question. She was now asking her questions out of pure curiosity rather than blind rage.

"Your current reaction seems to answer your question," Emma responded without missing a beat. Everyone knew that the question was more rhetorical than serious, but Emma wasn't always keen on nuance. The answer was obvious. Leo, Lyra, and Orion didn't want to upset Cassie. They planned to operate in secret for as long as possible.

"Yeah, you would've stopped us the moment you learned about it," Orion said, immediately agreeing with his aunt. He wanted to better convey his message, and Emma was the perfect medium for that. His additional comment rode off of hers and cleared away any misunderstandings. Granted, Cassie had no way of stopping her three siblings even if she knew about their actions, so maintaining the secret wasn't necessary.

"Since you've got your phobia, we knew you wouldn't join. So, it was better to not tell you at all," Lyra said, offering her own justification.

The reasoning was sound. Cassie couldn't deny that she was hesitant to join a group that frequently fought against Primals. The fear that gripped her would likely get her or someone she cared for killed. That was where the group's secrecy became a problem. A noticeable event like death wouldn't go unquestioned.

"What if you died? What did you plan to tell me then?" Cassie asked with a look of concern. Evolved-on-Evolved violence was typically avoided because it left both parties critically damaged. It was even worse when it came to Primals, who had mutated and held little value for their own life. This left the Celestials planning every operation to the fullest extent. If they didn't, they risked losing everything.

"We make sure to avoid that, but it's always a possibility. Protocol dictates that immediate family is alerted and life insurance would be dispensed. Of course, alternative causes of death would be written if it wasn't obvious that a Primal did it," Lyra said as if she was reading the words off of a memorandum. As a team leader, she knew everything that would've happened in any given scenario. The Celestials tried their best to be prepared for anything, even their demise.

"So, I would just go on with life thinking that you died from something else? Without ever knowing the truth? What the hell is the matter with you?!" Cassie shouted. All of her anger returned in an instant. Her siblings were insane. They had to be. There was no other way to explain how they thought that was a good idea. The very thought angered Cassie. She'd be infuriated and devastated if that ever happened to her. Unfortunately, the truth was what she asked for, and it was what her siblings would deliver.

"It's not like it'd be a new thing," Orion said. His words crushed whatever trust remained with Cassie. She could almost feel her heart shatter. Of course, Orion had no ill intent when he said what he did. He simply wanted to come clean about everything.

"Orion…" Leo and Lyra said in unison. Neither of them intended to reveal that bit of information. They debated on telling her after a few years had passed to save her the added grief and certainly wanted to avoid the topic now. Cassie wasn't in the right state of mind. She came closer to breaking with each new reveal, and no one was sure when she'd reach the tipping point.

"What? Might as well air out all the dirty laundry while we're at it," Orion said, visibly confused. He thought it was best to say everything here and now. If they withheld any information, it'd only come back to haunt them. Thus, the family grew ever more divided. Leo and Lyra wanted to end the conversation and maintain what little respect they still held. Orion preferred to dispel every lie he ever told, and Emma just wanted to know more of the story.

"Are you referring to Orion's death via Primal?" Emma rhetorically asked. Her question implied its answer and completed the message Orion tried to deliver. She wasn't in the mood for a farcical dodging of the issue. If any point she was aware of came to light, she'd explain it herself to get it over with. "I believe Tartarus ordered you to pretend it was a car crash. Is that correct?"

"How did you-" Leo started to ask. His wide eyes stared at his aunt in astonishment. She was not supposed to know that. Only Celestials knew the real cause of death, and only the three siblings knew what the fake cause of death was. Emma should have been fed the same lies as Cassie, yet she was more knowledgeable than she let on. Of course, she would never explain herself.

"Irrelevant." Emma blankly stated.

"Tch. Everything's irrelevant with you..." Leo mumbled under his breath.

"Great. Great. Fantastic. My entire life is a lie, and my siblings are psychos that run around in masks killing Primals. Did I miss anything?" Cassie asked. She ruffled her hair in frustration as she began to pace around the kitchen. She thought she was going crazy. The number of lies and twists was staggering, to the point where she believed this was some new nightmare of hers. The solution was clear, but Cassie realized she had to point it out to the maniacs she called family. "Why don't you just quit the group?"

"Absolutely not," Orion immediately replied.

"Sorry, but not even you can make us leave," Leo added to his brother's comment.

"You can join if you'd like, sweetheart, but we refuse to do what you're asking," Lyra said, finishing the triple denial. All three of them felt the same way about the situation. They refused to leave the Celestials under any circumstances. It wasn't for the money because there was none. It wasn't for pride nor glory. This was for something bigger. Something that involved the last secret they withheld.

"Why?" Cassie asked. She stopped her pacing to stare at them. She knew this involved the last thing they weren't telling her, but she wasn't sure if she could stand learning about it. Not after all that had happened. Her family lied to her for many years. It made her think they didn't trust her. Now, they didn't even value her opinion on what should be done next. The simple question echoed in Cassie's mind. The answer must have been grand to cause this much turmoil

"Allow me to explain," Emma chimed in.

"Aunt Emma, this really should be-" Lyra tried to stop her aunt from interfering, but the words wouldn't come out. Saying she wasn't family would be extremely rude. It was also unfair to flatly say 'butt out' to her. Even so, like a naive child that had grown up too fast, Lyra thought that she and the others could handle this alone. It was a sweet thought but also one that could be swiftly broken down by any reasonable adult.

"A family matter? Please. You are getting nowhere. I will talk to her. Alone," Emma said coldly. Her words cut deep and made everyone realize how circular the conversation was. Expose. Reveal. Question. Rinse. Repeat. If Emma stayed quiet, this would go on for hours with no progress being made. A single gesture sent the three unmasked Celestials away, leaving Cassie alone with her aunt for one final question.

"Why bring me here?" Cassie asked her aunt. The two were standing in the house's cluttered garage. Cardboard boxes were filled to the brim with mementos and hand-me-downs. Unfinished projects littered the area, and plastic containers held unused final products. Everything within the room was a fragment of the lives that were lived long ago. No one remaining wanted to clean this place, so dust and cobwebs engulfed the memorabilia. Adding to the age of the room, its concrete floor was heavily cracked due to foundational issues.

"Be silent," Emma commanded before commencing her search. What she was looking for was unknown. She refused to answer any questions and simply barged into the room with Cassie in tow. The two waltzed around the room as Emma glanced in all directions. She stopped at a few items, but only to remember the memory associated with them. She knew Cassie's parents well and missed them greatly. Unfortunately, gushing over memories wouldn't assist in the search.

"If you're looking for something, I can help you find it. I just need to know what it is," Cassie said. She didn't have a perfect inventory of the garage, but similar items were often kept together. It wouldn't be hard to find anything if she could associate it with a certain category. Honestly, Cassie just wanted to be of assistance in any way. She hated being forced to do nothing. Each fond memory that assaulted her vision swiftly became corrupted with thoughts of betrayal. She wondered exactly when her siblings became Celestials and so forth.

"You would not know. There is also the chance that it was destroyed." Emma mumbled. She didn't bother to stop her search and explain further. Her focus was solely on finding some mysterious object that eluded Cassie. In this state, it was almost impossible to snap her back into reality. Fortunately for Cassie, there was one thing that would wake her aunt from this trance.

"Something we're not supposed to know about? In that case, it's probably in one of the two trunks," Cassie commented. There were many things she knew about but even more that she didn't. Those gaps in her insight were well documented because she always wanted to return and solve those mysteries.

"Trunks?" Emma asked as she stared at her niece in disbelief.

"Yeah. When we were cleaning out dad's room, we found this ginormous trunk tucked underneath his bed. The thing was really heavy and locked though, so we just shoved it here and put it with the other one," Cassie said. She remembered most of the details because the event was recent. She could vividly picture the trunk in her mind. It was large and annoying to move. Any attempt to open it and reveal its contents was thwarted by a tedious lock. Even when the children got desperate, they couldn't break it open. Thus, it was shoved away and forgotten.

"They were never opened and disposed of? Both of them? Typical. Where are they?" Emma said. She would have appeared irritated had she the capacity to do so. Her guess should have had a low probability of being accurate, but it seemed that even she was due for a surprise. Emma only took the chance because of Tartarus. If he still had his old equipment, there was a high likelihood that others did as well. It was yet one more thing that linked the four of them together.

"I don't get what you're saying, but they're in the corner over here. I've got to warn you though, they're password-protected and stronger than even dad's armor. You won't get in easily," Cassie said with a perplexed expression. It was the first time she'd ever heard of those trunks needing to be destroyed. She certainly never heard of a way to open them, either.

Emma and Cassie walked over to the large boxes in the far corner of the garage. Both were made of a dark metal, and their edges were heavily reinforced. A large panel sat where a latch would and illuminated upon approach. Normally, it was difficult to move a single container, but Emma did so with ease. Cassie was left astonished as her aunt tapped both trunks' screens simultaneously. The bright blue panels shifted to a darker shade, and an echoed voice called out.

"SYSTEM ACTIVATED. WELCOME, USER," the machines said with monotone voices that rivaled Emma's. It was a phrase that Cassie had heard far too many times. It was the standard welcoming message that played every time someone tried to open the box. At one point, the voice almost had a mocking tone to it. Each attempt made the message grow more annoying until the four siblings eventually gave up on the ordeal. The trunks were pushed into the garage and forgotten, even by those who knew the truth.

"System override. Protocol: user expiration. Alternative user, Gaia, requesting transfer of privileges. Admin key phrase: echo victor charlie mike delta." Emma said without a moment of hesitation.

"OVERRIDE CONDITIONS MET. WELCOME, GAIA." The machines replied to correct phrases.

It was a stunning experience for the sole person who'd never heard anything other than denial from these devices. Cassie was at a loss for words. The spoken phrases were like something out of a dream, yet Emma made the impossible possible without the slightest bit of effort. She had the answer. She always did.

"What the-" Cassie stammered as the boxes opened before her. Its suspense had been building for years. Curiosity always gnawed at the back of her mind, but nothing could have been done at the time. Now, she was finally seeing yet another truth. One that her parents had hidden away for decades. Shock and awe filled Cassie as she saw the trunks' contents. She couldn't help but gasp at what was presented.

Both lids opened automatically and in unison. They retracted back and pressed against the wall while the central floor panel raised slightly at an angle. The first box revealed an amber suit with a matching tie and dress shoes sitting next to it. Each item was perfectly folded with care and placed on both sides of the container, making room for the jaw-dropping centerpiece. It was a mask. One that Cassie never thought she'd see. The base was bronze with a diamond-shaped plate welded over the mouthpiece. Covering the eyes was a frilled masquerade mask that was hand-painted. The eye holes were covered with a dark film, and the right eye hosted a large vintage camera lens. Numerous etchings of film reels filled the remaining empty space.

The second box opened in much the same way the first did. This one contained a red suit with a crimson tie and dress shoes. Unlike the other box, this one didn't have a lustrous mask. Instead, it carried a compressed motorcycle helmet. Its brilliant shade of red complimented the golden visor excellently and automatically drew attention. Small details were etched into the material, and white paint was used to make those images further stand out. Most of it was rather generic. The helmet depicted a typical night sky with a crescent moon and various stars that formed familiar constellations. To be specific, they were the Leo, Lyra, Orion, and Cassiopeia constellations.

"This is who your parents were. The Mobile and Armored Battalion Commanders: Nyx and Erebus," Emma said. With the key items present, it was impossible to deny what was said. The uniforms were one of a kind, crafted by Gaia herself. Everyone who lived through the Night of A Thousand Blades could attest to that fact. The commanders were known worldwide. Their names and masks were taught at schools so that no one forgot what had happened that night. What was in front of Cassie should have been in the most prestigious museum possible.

"No way…" Cassie uttered. She couldn't say more. Not even in her wildest dreams did she imagine a scenario like this. Her parents always seemed like the farthest thing from the people that participated in that night. They were kind and soft-spoken. They taught their children to avoid conflict and stay safe. If they had any part in that event, they'd have to be with the Support Battalion. That particular group helped humans during the crisis. That was a much more fitting role for the parents Cassie remembered, not some indestructible monster and an elusive threat.

"Shocked? I will give you a moment to recuperate," Emma said before taking a step back. This was a grand reveal, but she couldn't comprehend what her niece was experiencing emotionally. Emma had never been betrayed. She knew the answer to every secret. Her sideline view was the perfect way to watch everything unfold from a distance while still guiding the family along. All that was left was one more push.

Meanwhile, Cassie stood in silence for what felt like an eternity. Thoughts made their way through her mind, but most were lost in the abyss. Only two were prominent enough to linger. The first was her familiarity with battalion commanders. She knew her parents, who were both powerful leaders in their own right. Tartarus was next. He knew about her private life as any family member would. It now made sense as to why. He was like an estranged uncle to the four siblings. After all, it wasn't a secret that the commanders were close. They were almost like family.

The second thought was how this revelation affected her siblings. Those three were following a legacy while carving out one of their own. As children of commanders, they felt duty-bound to continue working until all Evolved could live in peace. Working on their father's project seemed to be the best way to do so, and Tartarus's assistance only bolstered them further. The other Celestials must have felt something similar from their own connections and joined as well, leading to the formation of a new generation of masked vigilantes.

"So, this is why…" Cassie mumbled. Though muddled with lies, the story was becoming clearer. The twins wanted to prove themselves to both of their parents that left them behind, and Orion wanted to honor the name he received from his late father. Only Cassie remained to decide her fate. Of course, there was still one more question that burned within her. She had been dying to ask it for years.

"Who are you?"

"Is that not obvious? It seems I gave you too much credit. Allow me to explain. I am the Support Battalion Commander. Designation: Gaia," Emma said, finally answering the age-old question. Her identity had finally been revealed. Although Cassie should have been able to guess the answer at this point, Emma was at the center of every conflict.

She exchanged information with Tartarus, and the two went their own ways when raising their nieces and nephews from the sidelines. One wanted the young to etch their names in history and better the world. The other wanted them to enjoy what the previous generation always dreamed of having. Emma cleared her throat before turning to her niece. She had a question of her own. "Now, who will you be?"

Chapter 6: Nova

Certain points of the Red Zone were notorious for their darkness at night. The zone's lack of funding led to lower development, leading to even more of these dark areas. These particular regions of the zone were also uninhabited and avoided at night. Consequently, the lack of people and patrolling vehicles was inviting to anything that wanted to avoid social scenarios. It was only by some miracle that the newest resident hadn't hurt anyone since that fateful night. Enforcer Romeo was the sole victim of this menacing Primal. Hopefully, he'd be the last.

Light was almost nonexistent in the nearby construction area. Only the moon and stars provided a semblance of illumination, but that wasn't an issue for the people that lingered in the darkness. Tartarus stood on an incomplete rooftop alongside Nike and Hemera. The three decided to rendezvous before their mission commenced to exchange information one final time.

"Hey, boss. Seems to me like that Cassie girl is a no-show. Should we assume she's not coming?" Nike said nonchalantly. The group had given their potential new member time to weigh her options, but their patience was limited. They had discovered where the Primal was and needed to act immediately. The mission would proceed as planned, minus the aerial support.

"Yes. I suppose it was too soon to make such a request of Cassiopeia," Tartarus said with a somber voice. He regretted how he pushed the child to do something she wasn't ready for. Her fear was a formidable foe, and Tartarus was essentially asking the impossible from her. No doubt Cassie was torn between following a battalion commander or self-preservation. He felt guilty for approaching her as his veiled self. He could have helped her in a much different way much like a friend of his did, but it was too late for that. The cards had been dealt, and the game must go on.

"I don't think the timing was the issue, sir. I believe it's simply that her fear runs deep." Hemera said. Naturally, Lyra felt awful about the situation, but she cast away that identity and its issues when her mask veiled her. A critical operation demanded her attention. She had no time to worry about trivial matters. Whatever needed to be done could wait until morning. Right now, Hemera and her duties required her full attention.

"That could be the case. It's also just as likely that her familial situation grew too stressful to make a proper decision," Tartarus said, staring at Hemera. He was told about everything that happened earlier in the day. She, Thanatos, and Hypnos had been chased out of their home by their aunt. They explained in great detail why they couldn't return, and Tartarus promptly gave them a stern lecture. He put the three on stand-by and speculated as to how the two rogue agents would react. Cassie was likely frantic, and Emma probably had a scheme up her sleeve.

"I'm sorry. Did I miss something in the report? Or are you creeping on a college student and her family?" Nike asked. Her heavy sarcasm hid how uninformed she felt about the potential new member. Despite being a team leader, she had no involvement in Cassie's recruitment. It was Tartarus that brought her and approved her release without any sort of insurance measures. Cassie could have easily gone to the police or informed the Enforcers, but Tartarus didn't worry. He placed as much trust in her as he did any Celestial. Now, he was discussing her familial situation with Hemera, who was supposed to be Nike's equal. It all left Nike feeling neglected.

"It's nothing. Let's move on. Have the preparations for tonight been completed?" Tartarus asked. He turned to see the view before him. A tall, partially constructed, building stood at the center of a grand open area with smaller ones surrounding it. This was once planned to be a central clock tower that overlooked a bustling plaza full of locally-owned businesses. Unfortunately, all that remained of that ideal project was its skeleton. It was scrapped due to lack of funding and left to crumble over time.

"Almost. The canisters are in place, but Gemini needs more time to get into position. Hypnos and Iris have prepared the nearby rooftops and are waiting for the signal. Then, there's Thanatos who's on standby in case the Primal tries to run," Nike said. She pulled out a small tablet to reconfirm the messages that were sent to her. Everyone carried theirs and relayed information to each other.

"Nike and I will also line the perimeter to complete the cage. Operation Canary will be ready in T-minus five minutes when the canisters pop automatically." Hemera said, continuing where Nike left off.

The operation was spearheaded by both team leaders who spent a great amount of time combing over the plan. There was only one chance to eliminate the Primal. If they failed, it would need to feast to recover and would likely relocate its nest in another zone or city.

"Good. I'm proud of what you've done without my guidance. As per your request, I'll stay here and watch your work, but I will step in if things get too dangerous." Tartarus said. He was happy that his subordinates were eager to show their growth, but a fine line existed between bravery and foolishness. Pride filled within Tartarus. He thoroughly analyzed the Celestial's plan and applauded their effort. The next generation was quite promising.

"Interesting. You are willing to sacrifice yourself for the children. Even though they yearn for death? Are you even capable of fighting at your old age?" A voice said from the darkness. The three Celestials spun on their heels and were greeted by the sight of a stranger. It was a tall and slender woman. She wore a tailored forest suit that sharpened her figure, and a fascinating gem mask covered her face. With a base of bort and eyes of emerald, the mask heavily resembled a spider's head.

"Support Battalion Commander, Gaia. I was under the impression you didn't approve of this group, yet you'll interfere with our operation?" Tartarus said with a somewhat irritated tone. He knew who she was based on her voice and odd speech pattern alone. He couldn't help but let out a defeated sigh. Emma was supposed to be accompanying Cassie at the moment. The poor girl was likely still reeling from the recent revelation. She shouldn't be left alone under any circumstances.

"I do not care about the Celestials. I care for my family. Something I feel you cannot relate to," Gaia said as she stepped forward. She analyzed the trio before her. Given her previous role, she was keenly aware of Tartarus and his abilities. The two women with him matched the descriptions that were given to her. The person in the knight helmet was the invisible woman. The other individual was her niece, one of the three children she took care of who didn't know her true identity.

"Family?" Hemera stammered. She was in disbelief at the woman that had arrived. She had never met Gaia before but felt an odd connection to her. Of course, Gaia's interesting voice gave away her identity. The reveal was alarming but also somehow refreshing. Hemera never knew her aunt had an alternate persona like her parents did. Something about the turn of events brought a bit of warmth to her heart. This truly was a family business, even if it did involve dangerous feats. The only thing that could have made this better was if Cassie was involved, but Hemera knew that would never happen.

"You are Hemera? How fitting. You followed mythology and chose the name of a deity who was born of Erebus and Nyx. I assume the others followed a similar theme?" Gaia said, teasing her niece. She fondly remembered when the original commanders took the monikers of primordial deities from mythology. It was a theme that tied the group together and acted as a subtle metaphor in the sense that they were creating a new world.

"Well…" Hemera began, then failed to complete her thought. Emma's accurate guess was extremely embarrassing. Lyra stressed herself when selecting her alternative name. She even studied to find names that coincided with old tales. At one point, she considered simply taking one of her parents' titles but quickly denied that idea. She was neither an armored-type like Erebus nor a mobile-type like Nyx. An assault-type like Lyra would only sully her parents' names.

"Why are you here?" Tartarus asked. He was happy to see an old friend, but spontaneous changes during such a vital mission could risk lives. She should have known that. If she wanted to help, Gaia should have arrived much earlier. Her ichor webs were impressive but required time to properly set up. She knew this, of course, which is why she had no intention of interfering.

"The same reason as you. I am here to watch the next generation. To see what they are capable of. Prove your worth, child," Gaia said, with emphasis on the word child. She turned to peer over her shoulder. The signaling key phrase had been spoken, and it was finally time for this weekend's victim to have a surprise of her own.

A figure shot out from the dark alley below. It darted from the ledge before Gaia and soared into the sky. They moved so fast that the two flares they held created a stream of crimson light. This shaded person dramatically flipped in the air before using their impressive wings to stabilize midair. Though the night was dark, there was enough illumination from both the stars and flares to see who this person was. She was a woman dressed like a former commander. She wore a rose suit with matching accessories and masked her face with a painted motorcycle helmet. Its golden visor gleamed in the light, and its red shell was almost begging to be a target. A beautiful night sky was depicted with white paint, and black wings were spray-painted onto the visor.

"It's nice to meet you all. My name is Aether. How may I be of assistance?" The woman said as she waved one of the flares in her hands. Her enormous wings ceased their flapping and dropped Aether to the ground. She gently landed next to Gaia, her mentor, and stood at attention. Aether's performance was certainly impressive, but no one was confused about who this was. Not even an altered voice could hide her identity.

"But she…" Hemera said with a low voice. She stressed over what to do. Her younger sister wasn't ready. Aether or Cassie or whoever she was had to go home. Hemera worried about giving a proper response. She wanted to immediately object, but that wasn't her call to make.

"This will be a trial by fire. Do your best," Gaia said with confidence. She was aware that this would be an uphill battle for her niece, but there was no better way for a bird to learn how to fly than by kicking them out of the nest. One way or another, she would learn to face her fear.

"I don't think-" Tartarus moved to say something but got cut off. Several metal clangs rang out in the hollow night. The subsequent angered hissing made the ground seem like it was full of snakes. The incomplete central clock tower was quickly engulfed with a dark haze. Too much time had passed, and Operation Canary had begun.

"We're not in formation!" Hemera shouted. She hadn't factored into account how much time was spent on the conversation. Gaia and Aether had distracted the three for too long. The canisters in the clock tower had already popped, so it was impossible to delay the mission. All other Celestials were enacting their roles in the operation. Hemera and Nike needed to hurry and complete the cage that the operation dictated. The Primal was bound to easily escape if two-thirds of the outer perimeter remained unsecured.

"Way to waste our time," Nike groaned at the newcomers. Her eyes audibly rolled with disdain. Everything would have gone smoothly had they never shown up. She was annoyed that the plan she and Hemera concocted was being thwarted by unknown variables. Her mind raced for a solution. If the commanders got involved, the operation would go perfectly. Unfortunately, that wouldn't happen.

"It'll be alright. Aether, fly to Thanatos and await-" Tartarus tried to say before stopping. He wanted to position his newest subordinate in the most optimal position to prevent the Primal from escaping. She, on the other hand, had a different strategy in mind. Aether flew overhead. She gracefully held out her arms to spread her flares' light. Once over the plaza below, she retracted her wings and spiraled to the earth below.

⁙

Aether fell for several seconds. She could feel the deafening wind rush by, but it was different somehow. This was not a simple race. This wasn't an escape attempt that her life hinged upon. It was an endeavor that she had to face, and Aether, or rather Cassie, was prepared for it. She was eager to live up to the uniform she wore. As the successor of the late Mobile Battalion Commander, Aether was to become an unhittable target. One that drew the enemy's attention while everyone else whittled away its defenses.

With a final deep breath of courage, she extended her wings and landed with flair.

The central clock tower was cloaked by a dense plume of smoke. The haze was difficult to see through, so it was impossible to see the target. Thankfully, they made no secret of where they were. The Primal burst through the smoke with its arms around its face. It fell to the ground and rolled around in a blind panic as it desperately tried to get the substance off. Now that the two were close, Aether was finally able to see her nightmare incarnate.

This Primal was as far from a normal person as one could get. Its skin was scarred, and chunks of flesh were missing. Ichor covered the bulk of its body, though there were noticeable spots of visible muscle and bone. Anything that could identify the person was long gone, including their original gender. This was the final and worst stage of a Primal. Their bodily functions were essentially nonexistent, although they still hunted and acted on basic instinct. Its excessive amount of ichor was the sole reason it lived, but that too would soon diminish. This Primal would soon die regardless of Operation Canary's outcome. At this point, the Celestials were conducting a merciful execution.

"Long time no see. I think it's about time we finish what we started. For both of our sakes…" Aether said, mumbling the last part underneath her breath. It was extremely unlikely that the Primal could hear her. Creatures like this were only concerned about three things: fighting, fleeing, and feeding. It couldn't care less about what Aether had to say, if it could understand her at all. She shrugged and dropped the flares that had petered out.

With the AE smoke no longer burning its flesh, the Primal responded to Aether with a guttural roar that was unlike anything a normal person could produce. One of its arms extended and bubbled as lumps accumulated underneath its ichor flesh. Each mass burst like a blister, revealing numerous large shards. The other arm doubled in width before flattening with several snapping and crushing sounds accompanying its formation. One of its sides thinned and hardened to form an incredibly sharp edge that could cut most materials in two. The other end remained blunt to crush anything the Primal couldn't slash through. The hideous sword and shield were primed for combat, but one more modification was needed before the beast could be satisfied. The Primal's feet formed monstrous claws. Its legs reassembled to parallel those of an apex predator. It scratched the floor beneath it, testing its newest addition.

Alright, body. I'm counting on you. Don't lock up, Aether thought to herself. She analyzed her opponent. It had more Armaments compared to their first encounter, and it wasn't using any of the ones she was familiar with. How many times had it mutated? All of those brutal changes must have caused unbearable pain. That thought bothered Aether. Primals probably endured just as much suffering as they caused, but there wasn't much she could do now. She couldn't change its past. All she could do was end its agony.

After evaluating its opponent, the Primal moved toward Aether. Its upper body fell forward as its hind legs pushed with unparalleled strength. The blade arm fell back and prepared for a mighty swing while its spiked counterpart acted as a battering ram. The Primal's mouth was destroyed and unhinged. Aether almost expected venom to spew forth or razor teeth to form. Thankfully, neither happened. The Primal was done mutating and blindly charged forward, rapidly closing the distance between them.

Uh... Alright... We can move now! Aether thought to herself. The scared girl beneath the mask trembled. Even with this new false persona, her fear remained. Of course, it would. Why would a simple mask remove a lifetime of trauma? She thought she could be brave, but it was obvious that she hadn't grown as much as she had been led to believe. Although, that wasn't to say her efforts didn't bear fruit. Aether's wings twitched and shot down to propel their master out of the Primal's attack path.

The beast missed its target. Its wild eye followed her through the air. The blade arm missed its swing, so the Primal was left with little option but to strike with its other weapon. The heavy spiked shield sluggishly approached Aether. She knew it wouldn't reach her, but she also didn't want to take any chances. Her feet quickly backpedaled away from the monster. The impressive Armament came within a hair's length of colliding with its target. A sudden shift forward would have struck her if it weren't for the sudden appearance of a masked man.

"Pretty bold of you to join. Don't think that this'll be a party, though. You'll be killed if you keep hesitating," Castor said. He took the brunt of the attack that would have killed Aether yet suffered little damage. The worst that happened was that he was shoved back and his suit was shredded, but the fibers of his clothing restitched themselves together. Surprised by the new challenger, the Primal stumbled back in a panic.

"Hey now, don't disrespect her! You've got guts, girlie. I like your style!" Pollux shouted with glee as he crashed into his target. His claws dug into the Primal's ichor flesh and effortlessly tore through whatever armor it tried to generate. The beast roared in pain before throwing itself on the ground to crush the pest that clung to it. Pollux immediately hopped off his enemy, elegantly flipping in the air. He landed with a pose, but there was no applause. Aether was taken aback by his daring nature, and Castor had likely seen the feat enough times to no longer be impressed.

The Primal assessed the changing situation and prepared for a grueling match. It readied its blade and assumed a battle stance. More ichor spikes formed on its shield to deter any further defensive maneuvers. It narrowed its crazed eye to focus on the person it deemed as the greatest threat. An intimidating roar escaped it as a sign that it was ready for battle. It stepped toward Pollux and gnarled its decrepit teeth. The monster was eager to finish off its foes, but something stopped it from rushing forward.

A long piece of rebar shot through the Primal.

A gasp of air escaped the beast. It lurched forward to understand what had happened. A slow head turned to scan the heavens that dared to strike it down. Of course, this wasn't some miracle or act of a higher being. This was an attack from the figure that stood off in the distance. The person stood on one of the nearby rooftops. They were surrounded by standing rods of rebar and used their elongated arms as a makeshift slingshot. Aether gazed in astonishment. She thought she recognized a friend but was mistaken. This was yet another Celestial.

"The plan is that Iris and Hypnos hit that thing from a distance while we piss it off down here. Think you can handle it?" Castor asked his temporary teammate. He knew that she was still having issues, but the battlefield would only stay calm for so long. The Primal was bound to grow impatient and counter. Aether needed to decide what her role would be in this operation. Given her Armament, the only fitting role was as a decoy.

"I don't know," Aether replied. She was still unsure of herself. The only reason she managed to expertly evade the Primal was because of a random spasm. She couldn't depend on those to continue the battle. A developed team to fight alongside her was helpful, but the fear remained. The trembling sensation and frosted blood overwhelmed all of her other senses. She truly wanted to help, but what could she do? All she could think about was the monstrous Primal before her. One hit. That was all it would take to end her life.

"You'll be fine. You're supposed to be the new Nyx, right? So, act like her. Fly around like a maniac and focus on evasion. Pollux and I will act as your shield. With us around, that thing won't lay a finger on you. You have our word." Castor said with a reassuring voice. He laid out the plan in a concise way. All that he needed from Aether was a bit of trust. Trust that they would keep her safe under any circumstance. After all, that was why they were there.

"Exactly as he said, miss decoy! Let's try starting slow, yeah? All you gotta do is fly up and come back down. We'll handle the fun part. Ain't nothing to it!" Pollux said in an oddly inspiring way. He made the situation seem trivial. Aether knew how to get off the ground since she was a child. That much was easy. Pollux even made the Primal seem like less of a monster. Gemini could handle the beast. One brother had hyper-regeneration, and the other had powerful armor. They were perfect for their roles.

"R-right," Aether replied. She realized she was no different than everyone else present. Everyone's life was at risk in this operation. The only reason they weren't terrified was because they trusted each other. If they all played their roles perfectly, they'd end the night with zero casualties. Aether's happened to be dangerous in brief instances, but she was far from the worst off. Gemini had to take the brunt of the assault. They were counting on her to help alleviate that by acting as a tantalizing, yet unreachable, target.

"Take a deep breath, kiddo. We'll go on your mark," Castor said with a low voice. His words were both calming and terrifying. It was now up to Aether to start the battle. If she didn't, the Primal would move to strike first and catch its enemies off guard. Castor readied himself to sprint at a moment's notice. Pollux assumed a similar lunging stance, and Iris loaded another bar for launch. A single action would start it all.

Aether subtly moved her hands back. She grasped the flares that hung at her waist. A single flick of the wrist activated them, causing a small eruption of smoke and sparks. The Primal roared once again and stepped forward. Aether's wings thrust with all of their might and hurled her into the air. The Primal was unable to resist following the trail of light and the odd woman fleeing the scene. It watched her with unbreakable attention, curious to see what she was planning. Aether then retracted her wings and allowed her remaining momentum to carry her to the apex of her launch.

Pollux immediately initiated his attack. He clashed with the Primal and dug his claws into its flesh. It knelt and began to roll in an attempt to crush the pest attacking it, but Castor rammed into the Primal before the attack could connect. His full force was put behind the charge and knocked down everyone involved. Gemini quickly got up and jumped away from the target. The Primal stood up dazed, shaking the concussion out of its head. It wasn't sure which brother was the most prevalent threat. Of course, neither was as awful as the person in the distance.

A thick piece of rebar shot through the monster and pinned it to the earth. Seconds later, another projectile came crashing into the scene. The Primal panicked and pointed its shield to the source of the shots. It willed its mutilated ichor to extend further than it normally could to form a massive wall. The material hardened as the Primal used its other arm to slice away at the foreign objects that pierced it. The beast reacted quickly, thinking it was safe for the moment, but a third rod broke through and shattered a portion of the wall. Little options were left for the Primal. It needed to escape quickly. It had no choice but to tear off chunks of flesh to free itself from its makeshift cage. Several pain-induced growls were heard before the Primal ran away with an obvious limp.

"Oh! My favorite part! The chase!" Pollux shouted with glee. It wasn't clear if he was playing a character or was insane as he pursued the beast. The Primal retreated toward the incomplete clock tower. The lingering AE smoke made the structure impossible to hide in, so the fleeing monster aimed to run by it. The best option was to escape the range of whoever was sniping it. That way, it could better handle the two brothers and the flying pest.

"It's using the building as cover. I need to relocate!" Iris shouted. Her words were difficult to hear, but the others assumed that she was going to move anyway. A marksman was worthless if the target refused to exit cover. Thankfully, Iris was more than capable of quickly maneuvering to a new position. She utilized her extendable arms to swing around the buildings and pivot to her next spot.

"Clever girl," Castor said. He followed his delighted companion at a much slower pace, crashing into his enemy while its back was turned. The Gemini brothers took turns attacking and made sure to never give the Primal a free moment. Castor pummeled his target with an armored body. Pollux tore through his enemy's ichor flesh with his claws. They were immensely powerful attacks, and the poison he was delivering began taking its toll. Then, the ceaseless onslaught suddenly stopped. Both men jumped back, and the Primal was filled with a sense of déjà vu. It looked around in a panic before two arrows struck its back.

"Nailed it!" Hypnos shouted from one of the nearby rooftops. He was ecstatic to land both of his shots despite the target being alert. Gemini hopped back into the fray as their companion prepared the next shot. Meanwhile, Aether flew around and acted as a distraction. She saw the two arrows that protruded from the Primal's skin and felt sorry for the beast. She knew how awful it felt to have those projectiles inside of her. That plus the never-ending onslaught of attacks must have been brutal.

The Primal grumbled as it processed what to do. Naturally, its thoughts were far from advanced. The beast was likely on par with a dog that had been cornered. It was desperate, and tactics were far from its strong suit. The barrage of attacks that chipped away at its defenses wasn't helping either. A final struggle was approaching, and the Primal recognized that it wouldn't be the victor. The monster decided to forego its offensive armament to focus on defense. Both arms reformed to create large spiked shields. The Primal blocked each attack while slowly backing up. Occasionally, it would throw out a wild attack, but the motion was overstretched and crashed into the clock tower's wall.

Aether continued to fly around, vying for attention and noticed something odd. Each of the Primal's attacks showed no sign of restraint. It left itself open to attacks every time its arms struck the incomplete building. Aether assumed that this was nothing more than frantic flailing, but she felt uneasy. Her eyes glanced at the clock tower's wall. Gaping holes littered the first floor of the structure. Chunks were beginning to fall due to the lack of support. The interior and upper levels were a wreck due to the damage below. It wouldn't take long for the worst to happen. Aether's eyes widened as she realized this.

"Gemini! Get out of there!" Aether shouted. The duo stopped their attacks and hopped back. They turned to see what was wrong with enough confusion to be seen through their masks. They had no idea why Aether was panicking, but they weren't going to ask questions. She clearly knew something they didn't, though they were immediately enlightened as to what that was.

A loud crash rang through the night as the clock tower's fate was sealed. The nearby wall was destroyed, and the few visible support pillars were broken with a single strike from the Primal. It used its shields as heavy clubs to break everything in sight. With the tower's structural support lessening from each attack, the building shifted and creaked. Debris rained from the sky. Construction equipment clattered on the ground. Dust was thrown into the air with each fallen object, mixing with the lingering smoke to create a dense cloud.

Everything next happened in an instant. The building toppled. Nowhere was safe in the direction the clock tower fell. Its whole structure covered the surrounding area, and the incomplete upper levels crashed on the nearby rooftops. Gears of various sizes clinked and rolled around while the bells gonged upon impact. The dense cloud of smoke and dust swept the area, though its Anti-Evolved effects were lessened significantly. Unfortunately, Gemini failed to escape in time. The brothers were crushed beneath the mountain of destruction that the Primal caused, and the perpetrator was nowhere to be seen. Aether panicked and flew in circles.

"We're fine. Obviously!" Castor shouted out. His voice was mostly muffled from the debris, but the message was delivered. A hand emerged from the chaotic mess. He slowly moved chunks of material out of the way, eventually freeing himself. The frowning mask he wore was likely indicative of his current mood. As an armored-type Evolved, Castor was used to testing his defenses' limits, but he certainly didn't enjoy having a building dropped on him. His brother was no different.

"When I find that Primal, I'm gonna wring its neck! Just as soon as I get out of this. Castor! A little help please!" Pollux shouted. Fortunately, he wasn't covered in heavy debris that was difficult to move. Unfortunately, he was impaled with various bars and pipes which made it impossible to escape alone. The smiling mask on his face was far from how he truly felt. Pollux was in a great amount of pain, but the wounds would heal the moment the foreign objects were removed.

"Uh, guys! It's looking at- Oh shi-" Hypnos yelled. His scream was cut short by the sound of a large explosion. The aftermath was visible for all to see. A nearby rooftop erupted. Something large crashed into it as the projectile was flung into the distance. The Primal may not have been intelligent, but it was smart enough to recognize Hypnos as the one that was peppering it with arrows. The beast sprung onto the building's front and began to scale the wall.

"Moving to intercept," Thanatos called out. His figure swung onto the scene, exactly as Leo did during the race. His tail extended and whipped through the area to find anchoring points. It didn't take long for the eldest brother to rendezvous with his younger counterpart.

"Same here. I'll provide backup and assist Hypnos with his relocation. Prepare to move Operation Canary's cage." Hemera said, providing additional aid to the current plan. She knew better than to jeopardize the operation, but she couldn't help herself. The lives of her two brothers were at stake. Even if it was out of Hemera's character, Lyra needed to watch over her family. The rest of the Celestials were left in the dark and simply followed orders, looking to Nike for additional guidance.

"Understood. Gemini and Aether will-" Castor tried to respond to the team leader. He was about to order Aether to accompany Iris, but a large shadow stopped him. It was his newest teammate. She was ignoring everything and flying toward the frontlines with unwavering determination. Her wings angrily flapped, sending her higher into the sky. The flares she carried continued to burn brightly, and Aether prepared for the final battle.

⁘⁙⁘⁙⁘⁙⁘

The Primal utilized freshly formed hands to climb the building it had recently destroyed. It scrambled over the ledge and rolled onto the roof. The ichor beast gazed around to analyze the area. Its curiosity was immediately punished with several arrows lodging into its torso and temple. Hypnos stood at the opposite side of the roof with his arms pointed at the Primal. His suit had been reshaped to accommodate the 'D' shaped structures on his forearms. Both crossbows were preparing for the next volley of shots, but the Primal refused to wait. It sharpened its hands into claws before charging forward in a blind rage.

"On your left!" Hemera shouted as she ran onto the scene. There was no hesitation in her movements. A strong urge to protect her brother drove each step. She confidently approached the Primal before sliding under its reckless attack. Her unsheathed arm blades sliced across the monster's midsection as she passed through.

Hypnos fired multiple shots while diving away from the beast. He repositioned himself to minimize the risk of accidentally striking his companions. The barbed arrows that Hypnos now used took longer to create, but they were much more effective. They clung to his enemy and caused damage each time the Primal moved. Its claws dug at the

152

annoying objects that stung with each step. It crouched down and roared in frustration.

"Oh, shut it!" Thanatos shouted before landing directly on top of his target. He put all of his weight behind the stomp, slamming the Primal's jaw into the roof. Its mouth shut with a few unnatural crunches, and the ferocious bellowing was cut short. Thanatos's tail whipped around his body and stabbed into his victim's throat. Knowing what was to come next, he jumped away from his current spot. The Primal's back bubbled before large spikes shot out. The attack missed by a hair, and the beast was forced to recover without confirming a single hit.

Hypnos nodded to Hemera. It was their only chance to make a big move. Hypnos grabbed at his arm and yanked the next shot out of its holding position. An ichor rope tethered him to it as he threw it to his sister. Hemera grabbed the arrow out of the air, and the two ran toward the dazed beast. They raced by their enemy, allowing the ichor rope to catch on the Primal's neck. The two then darted around each other to form a knot. Their preparations were finally in place. Hypnos and Hemera gave one final nod before throwing themselves off the building.

The Primal couldn't resist the force around its neck. Its head snapped back. The weight had been shifted, and the beast was dragged down. It scraped on the roof before reaching the edge where the ichor rope tightened.

Hypno and Hemera dangled from the building's edge. They pressed their legs against the destroyed wall and pulled with all of their might. Hypnos tried his best to retract the rope while his sister resisted. One final roar escaped the Primal, but it was more of a yelp. The rope suddenly loosened a bit before completely releasing. Hypnos fully retracted his Armament, and the two were left in a free fall. They braced for impact, but something snatched them out of the air well before they hit the ground.

"Geez. You guys are heavy. Ever considered going on a diet?" Aether said. She held her siblings in each arm. Her wings flailed as they tried to support the sudden weight change. Aether wasn't used to carrying multiple people, so she had to land immediately. The three steadily rose as Aether circled the building.

"I agree. Hypnos, honey, I didn't want to say anything, but you are looking a bit heavier," Hemera said. Her smile may have been hidden, but it could be heard in her voice. She poked at her brother's stomach to emphasize her point. The two sisters giggled when Hypnos flinched from the prodding of his sensitive sides.

"I am getting a bit more muscle definition. Thanks for noticing," Hypnos said as he swatted away his older sister's hand. He flexed his arms to show that difference since joining the Celestials, but that only made the girls laugh louder.

The three continued their banter as they normally would without the masks. Aether eventually reached the roof, and the trio was reunited with their final sibling. Thanatos gave them a polite nod before turning to the lifeless Primal. It was resting on the roof. Its neck had been cut through, and the head rolled away from the body. Meanwhile, all of the summoned Armaments were slowly retracting until all that remained was a small decrepit unisex figure that peacefully rested on the ground.

"Having fun?" Thanatos asked. He wanted to move past everything that had happened recently by breaking the ice. Sure, he was rude to his sister, but it was only because he wanted to protect her. He never could have imagined that she would willingly face a Primal. Even if she didn't deal any lasting blows, the once petrified girl was displaying her growth. Leo had no choice but to recognize it. Now, the four siblings' comradery was back in full swing.

"More than you could imagine," Aether said. Her statement was heavy with sarcasm, but there was an element of truth within it. She was both mentally and physically exhausted from the fight. The embodiment of all her fears had stared her down. In her mind, it couldn't have died fast enough. On the other hand, this was a new and refreshing experience. Aether was able to work with a team and fulfill her father's dream alongside her siblings. She could wear her mother's suit and helmet with pride.

"I still remember our first mission. You should've seen Thanatos. He was shaking in his boots." Hemera said. She was gleeful to see the family together again. Her chuckles were hard to hide as the image of a much younger Thanatos came to mind. He had come a long way from the blubbering mess he once was. Back then, he was much like his younger sister. He also had a fear of Primals, but that faded with each successful mission and encouraging words from his father.

"I seem to recall you crying for Erebus," Thanatos responded. He also had fond memories and secrets that some would have preferred to have been forgotten. The twins joined the Celestials at the same time, so they both saw each other at their worst moments. Hemera was no different from her brother. In some ways, she was even worse than him and cried out for her parents.

"Whatever you guys faced, it wasn't this thing," Hypnos said. He wasn't trying to be facetious. Rather, he knew that this Primal in particular was unique. Not even he could boast of an initial encounter that was better than this. Tonight's Primal lived for a considerable amount of time. It killed an Enforcer, and the Armaments it summoned were nothing to scoff at. Aether must have had incredible misfortune for this to be her introduction into the Celestial's operations.

The four continued their banter for a short while, ignorant of the movement behind them. A loose strand of ichor was slithering across the roof. Its sluggish pace prioritized discretion as it moved. This was a last-ditch effort to reclaim what little life the creature had. Moving like a lizard's tail, the thread of ichor randomly searched for salvation.

And, to everyone's despair, it found it.

The Primal was revitalized. Veins, nerves, and more strands of ichor quickly swarmed the connecting line. The lax cord thickened with each reinforced layer. The body slowly stood, but the head was dragged along the ground. Open arms slammed together, and the ichor-covered creature's limbs reshaped. Prominent 'D' shaped structures formed along its forearms. Beneath that, a razor-sharp blade appeared and reached past each of the Primal's hands. The monster shifted its shoulders with audible cracking and popping. Suddenly, a tail ejected from its hindquarters. Its tip was curved like a sickle, perfect for both slicing and piercing. The Primal lurched forward and gargled its fluids. Ichor spilled from its mouth as the head slowly retracted back to its proper position. Then, two masses formed along its shoulder blades and bubbled before bursting to reveal newly created wings.

The Primal had perfectly replicated its opponents' Armaments.

"Does that usually happen? Cause I think I'm gonna stay home next time," Aether said. She fluttered her wings as if to make sure they were still there. Primals were known for mutating uncontrollably, but none had ever been documented with the ability to copy other people's Armaments.

"It's getting desperate and using the last of its ichor to adapt. Stay in formation and prepare for combat," Hemera said. She had resumed her team leader persona and stepped forward. Her bladed arms stood at the ready. The Primal's forced mutation may not have been as strong as its others, but this would still be an intimidating fight. Thankfully, the four siblings were fully aware of each other's Armaments. They knew how to work together as a cohesive unit.

"Yes, ma'am," The other three replied. Each readied their respective Armaments. Hypnos and Aether remained in the back row. Thanatos stepped forward to join his sister. How long had it been since they all fought on the same side? Probably when they were younger and charging at their father in a game of "can't get past me". It would have been a nostalgic moment, but this wasn't the time for reminiscence.

The Primal lunged forward. An intensive aura radiated from it. The beast knew it wouldn't be free until it took a life, so that was what it was planning to do. Both bladed arms were aimed at Hemera. She took the blow with her Armament and stared down the face of death. She pushed forward but quickly realized the danger she was in. She shoved her enemy away and stepped back, narrowly avoiding the arrows that fired from the monster's wrist. A second later and her head would have been skewered.

Unfortunately, that wasn't the last of the Primal's attacks. Its tail whipped along the ground to sweep everyone off their feet. The intimidating sickle scraped the roof as it dashed around but stopped suddenly. Thanatos had timed his stomp perfectly, crunching the formation beneath his boot. He knew the pain of having his tail stepped on, and it was audibly displayed by the Primal's yelp. That agony only worsened when Thanatos used his Armament to slice the false copy in two.

The Primal recoiled from the attack. It stumbled away and glanced around. These two enemies were accustomed to fighting. A prolonged encounter would not end well for the beast. This left only one logical conclusion. The Primal had to start its slaughter with the other two Celestials. One had wings and was incredibly difficult to reach when they took flight. The other was an annoying ranged-type Evolved that lacked a means of escape.

Perfect.

The Primal twisted to face Hypnos, the most annoying of the bunch. It was him that continually peppered the beast with arrows. He was the one that lobbed off its head. If the Primal could kill him, its struggle would dramatically decrease. Vengeance was also a driving factor, so it was no surprise that the Primal used its version of a rope shot. It intended to pierce Hypnos and drag him within melee range, where it would then rip off his head. A steady arm rose, and a bone bolt was fired.

Time seemed to slow as the arrow soared through the air. Aether, or rather Cassie, watched in horror. She felt the frost within her build as her worried eyes traced the shot's path. Within moments, it would collide with her brother. The resulting hit would have been fatal, if not detrimental. The four may have had their standard Nectar vials but that wasn't enough to patch a wound that significant. Something had to be done to save Hypnos' life. Someone had to step in.

Before she knew it, Aether was diving into the arrow's path.

Her body had moved on its own. Even she didn't know what was happening. This went against everything she knew and was ordered to do, but she refused to allow someone she cared about to be hurt. The roped shot lodged itself into her shoulder. It pierced her flesh and crushed her bones. This shot was much larger than anything Orion ever launched at her, and Aether immediately felt it pull her. She grasped the line with both hands to resist the motion, but the pain was unbearable. Her wings expanded and propelled her off the ground.

The Primal panicked as it was slowly lifted into the air. Its wings flapped to fight against Aether, but they were nothing more than large targets. Hypnos fired off multiple shots. Each arrow pierced the wings with ease, leaving large holes in their wake. The Primal's ichor was limited, so it couldn't rapidly regenerate the damage that was dealt. It couldn't fly nor could it latch onto the rooftop.

The two fiercely fought as they thrashed in the air. One held its victim without showing any sign of retreat, feeling every tug as it tore apart her shoulder. The other wanted nothing more than to return to the earth, but that hope was slowly diminishing with each passing second. The Primal decided to retract its ichor rope and slash at Aether once high enough. The beast slowly climbed up to the bird of prey that held it, but its movements were halted. A sharp pain rang through the

Primal's legs. Its head twisted to see what dared to attack it, only to see ropes of ichor were now attached to it. Hypnos had landed his shots and anchored his enemy. He nodded to his aerial sister before pulling with all of his might.

The Primal felt itself being pulled in two directions. Its arms were pulled toward the heavens while vicious chains dragged the legs to hell. Both forces fought valiantly but were equal in strength. The struggle went on, and the victim in the center of it all felt a tear forming. Its body wouldn't last long. Frantic thrashing did nothing but show how afraid the monster was. This trap was inescapable. The Primal roared in frustration.

Thanatos and Hemera watched the sight. They glanced at each other and understood what had to be done. The duo assumed sprint stances, waiting for the perfect opportunity. The Primal was continually bouncing around with each thrash. Timing was everything. As if they heard a starting pistol fire, the twins took off in unison. Each step propelled them forward. Their acceleration was impressive, launching them off the building with staggering speed. Hemera extended her arms. Thanatos spun in the air. Both aimed their Armaments at one vital point. At the same time, Aether and Hypnos pulled their enemy and tightened the rope to hold them still.

Then, it was ripped in two and silence encompassed the area.

Half of the weakened monster fell. The rest ascended into the sky. Aether knew the job was done, but she wanted the mission to be completed with a more ceremonious ending. One that better represented her growth. She soared into the air before suddenly stopping. The upper half of the Primal continued its course thanks to the momentum that carried it. The creature was still alive but not for long. It didn't even have the energy to resist Aether as she flew around it. The copied Armaments it had were quickly restrained by the Primal's rope.

Satisfied with her knot-tying skills, Aether took the liberty to jam the arrowheads that were once in her into the Primal. She grabbed the creature by its neck and used her other free hand to remove her helmet. Cassie locked eyes with the monster that haunted her. She could feel the fear filling her as her alternate persona took a backseat. A deep breath helped calm her nerves. She took one final look at the Primal. This was once an Evolved with friends and a family. This was once a person. One who was probably loved. One that was at death's door and needed to be properly pushed through.

With a shaking hand, Cassie loosened her grip and allowed her living nightmare to splatter on the ground.

Epilogue

Emma sat alone on a bench in an empty park. The sky was dark with heavy clouds that were bound to rain at a moment's notice. Luckily, she came prepared. An umbrella rested on her lap, ready to ward off the inevitable downpour. It was once considered good luck to have rain on a day like this, but Emma never believed in superstitions and old wives' tales. She had no intention of leaving, no matter the weather. She'd stay in the park until the figures across the street were done with their activities.

They were the four children she cared for in their parents' absence. All of them were dressed in black formal wear, mourning the anniversary of their loss. Each person held a single black rose that was purchased earlier in the day. They gazed down at the tombstones before them and gave a silent prayer. A deafening silence filled the air for several minutes before someone spoke.

It was Cassie. She told her tale to those who were unable to see it for themselves. Tear-filled laughs escaped the group when they discussed the ludicrous race and the following morning. Droplets full of emotion splashed on the ground as she recalled the reveal of her siblings' identity. Sniffling constantly interrupted the impressive story of the final battle. Cassie tried her best to tell her tale, but she couldn't finish the story. She fell to her knees and wept.

Emma continued to watch from a distance in silence. She saw the others comfort their little sister. It was a heartwarming moment. One that she wished she could have been a part of, but that would have to wait for another time. Emma still had to give her report to her fallen comrades once the children were gone. She didn't believe in an afterlife, but it felt like the right thing to do. It would be her final act as both a fellow battalion commander and a friend, along with a certain someone else's final performance.

"Have you been waiting long?" A deep voice spoke. It was an elderly gentleman with a northern accent. He sat next to Emma, taking care not to rustle his dark formal attire. He rested his cane beside him and stretched his legs. His short hair was combed to the side, though the rain would soon ruin it. Scars peppered his body, but most of his outfit covered the more gruesome blemishes.

"Fifteen years to speak to Nyx. Exactly one year to speak to Erebus. Three months to speak to Eros. Seven minutes to speak to Tartarus," Emma said. She didn't bother to look at the man who sat next to her. Instead, Emma's gaze remained locked on the grieving siblings. They were now all sobbing and apologizing profusely for various reasons. One wanted to visit the grave more often and vowed to live up to their given name. Another took responsibility for the recent affairs and swore to do better as one of the elder siblings. The third refuted every lie that was ever said, promising to protect the family from any ordeal. The last regretted denying help and said they would listen to the others.

"I can't say you'll get to speak to Tartarus. Brent is the person sitting next to you. There is a difference, Emma," Brent said with a slight chuckle. He sat back in his seat and prepared for the worst. His friend could give extremely long lectures if she chose to, and the two were at odds at the moment. One believed it was best to protect the children they were entrusted with. The other wanted them to grow through numerous hardships as the previous generation once had to. Aside from their differences, they wanted their nieces and nephews to grow up and pursue their dreams as any normal human would.

"It does not matter which name you use. Only two issues are up for discussion. The first should be obvious. I do not approve of your group," Emma said. The irritation was subtle yet noticed. It was far from a secret that she didn't like the concept of the Celestials. They were brutes that only operated to eliminate Primals and Fallen. Only a select few of them had sources that could cure the blight, but the group couldn't do it alone. None of them were equipped to fully remove the pressing issue that infected every Evolved.

"I know. I know… I also know that Nyx wouldn't have approved of it either. Eros…well, I'm not sure where they stand," Brent said. He was in a precarious position, much like Emma was. Half of the commanders stood against the team's formation while the other half was all for it. The only person that could break the tie, Eros, was off enjoying a luxurious retirement. Which was something all of the commanders should have been doing.

"I will allow you to continue operating out of respect for you and Erebus. It is not as if the project is completely useless. The children seem to be growing under your tutelage," Emma responded. She couldn't deny the results that Tartarus produced. The various charges that he was entrusted with changed in many ways. Cassie's phobia and nightmares were now tolerable. The twins had a newfound respect for their younger counterparts, and Orion was slowly becoming more confident. Equal praises could be given to the other children who were also delivered to Tartarus from numerous participants of the Night of a Thousand Blades.

"I'm glad. It'd be a problem if we fought any longer. I'm worried that some of the others might have gotten involved," Brent said. He recalled some of his old companions. It would be nice to see them again, but some of them had issues controlling themselves. One grew more wild as she fought while her partner followed suit to protect her. Another Evolved simply lived to be in the spotlight, and their companion acted in kind to keep them safe. If they got directly involved with the Celestials, it could spell trouble.

"My next concerns the voice. Veronica once confided in me about it pestering her. Her expiration came shortly after. I fear the same is happening with myself," Emma said. She recalled the conversation she had with her friend over a decade ago. A voice was constantly bothering the mobile commander, tearing her mind apart with each passing minute. It was a unique symptom that Fallen suffered from when they were descending into madness and becoming a Primal. Now, Emma could hear its voice. It was quiet, but its presence alone was mortifying.

Emma's time was limited, and she wasn't alone in that position.

"You too, huh? That makes three of us, including Morgan. What's yours been saying?" Brent asked. According to the currently known cases, different Evolved heard the same voice say different things. There was no noticeable correlation that connected groups to what was said, so it was surprising to hear that afflicted commanders were all receiving the same message.

"Submit."

Afterword

Somehow this part of the book is the most nerve-wracking part to write. Unlike the main story, I never know what to write here.

Obviously, I'd like to start by giving my thanks. Thank you to my wonderful family that supported me through the writing process and encouraged me to pursue this crazy dream of mine. The little suggestions and feedback given after my constant prodding meant the world to me (so be ready for more when you're done reading this). Even with the hectic life I lived during writing this, none of you doubted that I would finish this book. I'd also like to thank my friends for inspiring me and some of the characters in this story (feel free to figure out who). And, a special thanks to my friend Jesse for creating the awesome cover and recreating the cover for the original book.

The Next Generation tells an interesting tale about family, trust, and trauma. Hopefully, I did the story justice, but it is far from over! We've caught glimpses of how society has adjusted to the Evolved, but what happens when tensions rise and people decided to take a more radical approach? That's what a certain set of brothers will face in the next book! Oh! I can't wait!

Until then, thank you so much, again. I hope you'll continue reading.

See you then.

www.ingramcontent.com/pod-product-compliance
Lightning Source LLC
Chambersburg PA
CBHW070508200726
48293CB00007B/2452